# GYPSY

*A Promised Land Romance*

Other books by Carolyn Brown

*Love Is*
*A Falling Star*
*All the Way from Texas*
*The Yard Rose*
*The Ivy Tree*
*Lily's White Lace*

The *Promised Land Romance* Series:
*Willow*
*Velvet*

The *Land Rush Romance* Series

*Emma's Folly*
*Violet's Wish*
*Maggie's Mistake*
*Just Grace*

# GYPSY

•

**Carolyn Brown**

*AVALON BOOKS*
NEW YORK

Library of Congress Catalog Card Number: 2003097358
ISBN 0-8034-9646-X

Published by Thomas Bouregy & Co., Inc.
160 Madison Avenue, New York, NY 10016

PRINTED IN THE UNITED STATES OF AMERICA
ON ACID-FREE PAPER
BY HADDON CRAFTSMEN, BLOOMSBURG, PENNSYLVANIA

With thanks and appreciation
to my editor
Erin Cartwright-Niumata

## *Chapter One*

Tavish O'Leary pulled up his horse's reins on a *torr* and looked down at the bright campfires of the wagon train camp. Knowing he'd found the right train wasn't difficult. It would take a hundred women to produce that much fluttering laundry. With his short legs, he kneed the big roan horse and proceeded down the side of the *torr*. He'd go in quiet and surprise his Uncle Pat, who'd taken his place on the train for the past several weeks.

He crossed the river without making too much noise and was riding toward the flickering camp lights when he saw the Indian woman sitting with her back against a big tree. Her chin rested on her chest and her arms were dangling at an odd angle off to her sides, as if she'd just fallen asleep. Clouds covered the moon, and the stars produced very little light. Not enough to see if she was breathing or not, but it sure didn't look like it.

She had to be dead.

Someone had killed her and left her beside the tree. Possibly, the whole wagon train had been wiped completely out. He strained his ears to listen intently toward the wagons, and heard the soft hum of feminine voices. There was no way she could be part of the wagon train of brides, though. Hank Gibson would never sign on an Indian woman to take to California to a hundred bridegrooms who'd been waiting a whole year for the train to arrive with their mail order brides. No, sir, if those gold diggers wanted Indian brides they sure wouldn't have laid out the money they did to get them all the way from the Missouri to California.

He eased off his horse so quietly in the still night that his jeans brushing against the well-worn leather saddle barely made a sound, blending in with the night wind rustling through the trees. Clouds fluttered across the full moon, and finally there was enough light so he could see that she wore a faded calico dress and no shoes, her toes peeking out from under the hem. She hadn't moved, and Tavish still couldn't tell if she was breathing or not. Every hair on the nape of his neck stood straight up. Not even if a band of the good folk, the Irish fairies, came out from behind that stand of trees, and played their harps for him, would he touch a dead body.

Two long braids hung down either side of her chest like big, thick black snakes. Sitting there like that, it was hard to determine if she was a big woman or not. She looked short but Tavish had been wrong before. Several times when it came to women.

"Hey squaw," he said, and nudged her with the toe of his boot.

Instantly, the woman grabbed his leg, flipped him onto his back, was sitting astride his chest in a flurry of petticoats, and had the blade of a knife to his throat. He tried to swallow but his mouth was so dry that if he'd had to spit or die, he'd have to say his final prayers without the benefit of a priest.

"Who are you?" she asked.

"Who are you?" he found the courage to ask against the hot steel of the knife about to dice his Adam's apple. *Strange,* he thought crazily, *the metal is warm and not cold like most knives.*

"That's none of your business," she said. "Give me two

good reasons why I shouldn't slit your sorry throat right now."

"Because he's my nephew, and because he's going to help get this train on to Californy," Pat O'Leary said, stepping out of the shadows. "Guess he must have startled you, Miss Gypsy."

"You better work on getting him trained before you forsake us, Pat. He's rude and stupid." Gypsy sheathed the knife in a small leather pouch hidden in the folds of her skirt, which she gracefully whipped back so she could stand.

Tavish sat up, rubbed his neck to make sure there was no blood, and glared at the woman. "You better watch your mouth. I'm surprised Hank let Indians go with him on this train. There ain't a man in California who's going to want a squaw for a wife. They want decent white women."

Gypsy turned quickly and took a step forward, putting her nose to nose with the ignorant little short man. "Point proven. Stupid and rude! I'm not Indian. I am Gypsy Rose Dulan. I am half Mexican. My grandparents and my mother, before she died, are wealthy land owners and horse breeders in south Texas. My father was Jake Dulan. As if any of that is an ounce of your sorry business."

Tavish looked into the strangest colored eyes he'd ever seen. Even with only the light of the moon to illuminate them, they were the color of a robin's egg. Not blue like a summer sky or even green like the plush grass of Ireland, but something in between. Like they'd been blessed with the warmth of the color of green, and kissed with the coldness of blue. One thing for sure, she was Jake Dulan's daughter, all right. She had his eyes and more than her fair share of his quick temper. "Well, accept my apologies, Miss Whatever-your-name-is. You look like an Indian to me."

"And you look like a little boy to me. You better get him out of my sight, Pat, before I take my knife out and cut this child's throat just for waking me up in the middle of a good dream," Gypsy said, picking up her boots and taking off at a fast walk toward the circle.

"You're not big enough to cut my throat," Tavish threw out at her back.

She turned around so fast he wondered if she'd ever been walking away from him. In a few easy strides she was so close to his face that she could feel his warm breath on her soft neck skin. Something deep in her belly tightened up. Anger. Pure, unadulterated rage, she figured. "You're not old enough or big enough to be putting down another person. If you are a day past sixteen, I'll eat my boots. And don't you ever underestimate me. I could take this knife from my skirt and send you to eternity so fast you'd wonder if you'd ever walked on this earth, little boy."

"You better start chewing on those boots, lady. I'm twenty-five. Just because I'm short, don't you underestimate me, either," Tavish growled.

"Children, children," Pat laughed. "Enough now. 'Tis time you got on back to camp, Miss Gypsy. Your sisters were worryin' about you is why I came lookin' anyway. And it's time you come with me, Tavish. Come and give your old uncle a hug, and we'll settle down with a cup of good hot coffee. Tell me, have you heard from the folks? I haven't had word in six months and I'm eager to get home. Hank's been expectin' you for a week or more. Me, I'm glad to see you."

Gypsy flaunted off toward the light of the camp without a backward glance. So this was the nephew Patrick O'Leary spoke so highly of on a daily basis. That meant he'd be riding at the rear of the train and she'd have to look at him every day. She'd rather face down a coiled rattlesnake with nothing but a lace handkerchief for a weapon. Still fuming when she reached her wagon where two of her sisters, along with Annie and her adopted daughter, Merry Briley, waited, she slammed her boots in the wagon, picked up her bedroll and slung it out under the wagon. Lord, what on earth had made her think she wanted to ride a wagon train of more than a hundred women from St. Jo to California?

"What's the matter with you?" Garnet, her sister asked.

"Short men. They're all so full of themselves," Gypsy hissed.

"Hey, what's going on?" Gussie asked from the other side of the wagon.

"Gypsy's been out there searching for secrets in her stars, and came into an almighty prophetic revelation," Garnet said. "She's determined that short men are full of themselves."

Gussie laughed, a deep, rich laugh. "So you finally found out what the stars have to say. You could have asked me or Garnet about men, especially short ones, and we could've told you that. Did those stars rearrange themselves in the sky and write that out for you or did you just come up with it on your own?"

"Oh, hush," Gypsy said.

"Who is that?" little Merry Briley asked, pointing toward Pat O'Leary and his nephew circling the wagon train and heading toward the small camp the men had made about 20 yards away.

"Could be that's the source of Gypsy's revelation," Garnet said. "Want to tell us about it?" she asked, brushing her long red hair its hundred strokes before she braided it for the night.

"He's Pat O'Leary's nephew. The one who's coming to ride at the back of the wagon train. To keep all those mean Indians and trail pirates from picking us off and selling us into slavery. As if that little boy could rescue a kitten out of a tree. He's short, bow-legged, stupid and rude, and that's naming his best qualities. He's nothing more than a boy even if he is twenty-five-years-old. He'd just better stay out of my way or next time I will cut his throat and leave him for the buzzard's breakfast. Calling me a squaw. Lousy, ignorant short man. Doesn't have a lick of sense."

Gypsy beat her pillow into submission and threw her head down on it with a thud. "Good night. I'm going to sleep."

"Called you a squaw?" Annie asked. "What made him do that?"

"Came upon me sleeping. My hair is in braids. I guess any woman who wears braids and falls asleep next to a tree is a squaw. Fool, anyway."

"Whew!" Gussie wiped the back of her forehead with her hand. "I'd say that boy and Gypsy done got off on the wrong foot. Wonder why he'd call her a squaw. Is he so blind he can't see her eyes or her beauty?"

"Does that mean Uncle Pat will be leaving?" Merry Briley said, as her seven-year-old eyes welled up with tears. "I'll miss him."

"We all will, but I betcha Gypsy and his nephew keep us well entertained," Gussie said.

"If he lives that long," Garnet added.

Gypsy snorted but she didn't open her eyes or comment. Tavish O'Leary had better learn right quick to stay out of her way. She flopped over and opened her eyes to look at what stars were visible from under the wagon. The old gypsy woman, Paqui, who'd been her mother's friend first and her own friend later, said there were secrets up there. She told Gypsy just before she left south Texas that if she studied them she'd find the secrets. Gypsy had sneaked away from the wagons to study them earlier that evening when she'd fallen asleep. Then Tavish woke her rudely with the toe of his dusty old boot. There hadn't been a secret fall down from the moonlit, star-struck night into her lap as she leaned against the big oak tree beside the river.

Maybe the secret was that she needed to quit this nonsense and go home. With very little persuasion she could probably talk her older two sisters into going with her. She hadn't been real happy lately, and thoughts of looking at Tavish O'Leary all day surely didn't bring on any giggles. She'd quit this wagon train and go on home to south Texas. Abulita, her short little grandmother, might fuss but she'd be glad to see her. It wouldn't take Gypsy more than half a day to be back in her good graces, especially if she brought the beautiful red-haired Garnet and lovely golden-haired Gussie with her. The men in south Texas would fall all over themselves to get near those two beauties.

How in the world did she go from being a pampered rich Mexican horse trainer to walking 15 miles a day with a wagon train of more than 100 mail order brides? She sighed, thinking back to April of that year. There were five Dulan sisters who met in St. Joseph in the spring of 1860, every one of them hoping to talk to their father, Jake, before he died. None of them got that privilege. They'd all arrived in time for the funeral, and when the will was read, found out there were five Dulan girls. All with different mothers, but all sharing the same strange blue-green shade of eyes. Jake, along with his partner, Hank, had planned to take a wagon train of brides to Bryte, California. The pay was double what they usually charged, and was going to be their last trip. The sisters made a deal with Hank. They'd sign on with the train to be his insurance. If, when the journey ended, there were more than 100 women alive, they'd step back and let the other women have the husbands.

They'd lost three women already. One died with a fever, the same one that made Pat O'Leary take Velvet Dulan to Fort Laramie and leave her with the doctor there. Gypsy wondered how her sister, Velvet, was faring, now. Had she died or was she already on the next train and would join them in Bryte?

Willow Dulan, the youngest of all the girls, had bowed up to Rafe Pierce, one of the hired hands who had helped on the train during the first leg of the journey. The one from St. Jo to Ash Hollow, where Pat O'Leary joined it for the next bout in the journey. Sparks flew between Willow and Rafe until the day he rode off to his ranch in Nebraska. A few days later he rode back into their midst to declare his love for Willow, marry her right then on the spot, and take her away.

Two sisters already gone. Three left. Gypsy, Garnet and Gussie. Garnet had always said she wouldn't marry anyone at the end of the trail. Gussie said she would because she wanted a family someday and she wasn't getting any younger. Gypsy didn't want to marry someone whose name was drawn from a hat when they got to California. Lord, she'd just have to lay down and die if Hank drew a name and there stood some short little, egotistical man with bowed legs and an attitude as big as Tavish O'Leary's.

To stand right there in front of her and say he wasn't afraid of that knife to his throat . . . that was a bald faced lie. She could smell the fear in his eyes when she had him on his back, arms pinned to his sides with her knees. No, sir, she most certainly did not intend to marry a short man. She wasn't sure if she ever wanted a husband. But if she did fall in love someday it would be with a tall blond-haired man with nice twinkling blue eyes.

She sure didn't want a boy playing like he was a man. Nor did she intend to fall for some Irishman with black hair and mocking black eyes. She sat up, bumped her head on the undercarriage of the wagon and bit her tongue to keep from yelling out in pain. Tavish had caused her to hurt her head. If it hadn't been for his caustic insults, she wouldn't be angry at the whole world. She had no trouble with the fact he'd called her a squaw, not in the least. Indians weren't all that different than Mexicans or white folks. They lived a different lifestyle but so had Mexicans back centuries ago. It was the sneer on his face and the tone of his voice that told her what he thought of anyone whose skin wasn't as pretty and pale as his. Because that was the only difference between them. His hair was black; hers was black. His eyes were even darker than any Indian's she'd ever seen, and hers were blue. So there, Tavish O'Leary! What kind of name was Tavish anyway? Maybe she had the right to kick him with the toe of her boot and call him an Irishman in a derogatory tone. If he'd just let her sit there in peace, she would have awakened in a few minutes. She wouldn't have even known him until tomorrow. Now, she was riled up, and Gypsy always had trouble sleeping when she was riled.

Little Merry Briley's chin quivered, and tears flowed unashamed down her little freckled cheeks. Gypsy could have cried for her if not with her when Pat O'Leary mounted his horse and rode off to the south. Merry had had enough heartache in her young life. Her aunt and uncle had taken her in when her parents died. They'd taken her along when they joined a wagon train and were on their way to California when they were beset by highway pirates and everyone killed but Merry. Willow had found her whimpering and bewildered and brought her back to the camp. She recognized Annie from the week she and her aunt and uncle had stayed in the Patee house where Annie, along with several other brides, had stayed after they'd signed on with Hank's train of women. So Annie had taken her under her wing and after three months, no one questioned the fact that Annie was her mother.

Today, though, Gypsy had trouble keeping her own chin still as she watched Pat disappear. Merry would miss him because he'd been a surrogate uncle to her, often letting her ride on his horse with him, entertaining her with all kinds of Irish folklore and stories. Gypsy would miss him because she already didn't like his replacement. His nephew—Tavish O'Leary.

"Dry them tears, my pretty lass," Tavish said, patting Merry's shoulder. "Uncle Pat said I could be your uncle now. You can call me Uncle Tavish and today, I have an Irish song to teach you. That is if you'd be kind enough to ride with this old man on his horse. A pretty little lass like you, even with freckles where the Irish fairies have kissed you in your sleep, shouldn't walk today. Not with tears flowing down your cheeks. You must be careful, crying like that, Merry, my lass. All those tears might wash away the angel's kisses and make them sorry they kissed you in your sleep."

Merry looked up in awe. "You ain't old enough to be an uncle. You're just a little boy."

Gypsy laughed, her blue eyes sparkling in mischief. "Out of the mouths of babes, I'd say Mr. O'Leary."

"Tavish. Mr. O'Leary is my father, my grandfather and my uncle. I'm Tavish, no matter whether you like me or not, Miss Dulan," he said, coldly.

His black eyes glittered with annoyance and she stifled another giggle. In the light of early morning she could see that he was indeed 25-years-old. His strong jaw sported shadows of a heavy beard even though he'd no doubt shaved the night before. Yes, he was a man, a fine looking one at that, but his height sure made him look like a little boy, even to Merry.

"You know what, Miss Merry, I've got a niece who's even older than you are. She's thirteen-years-old, and she rides like the wind. She has red hair and freckles where the Irish fairies kissed her too. Her name is Meagan," Tavish said, ignoring the flippant Mexican beauty. Mercy, how could he have ever mistaken her for an Indian woman? Her features had been carved from the finest porcelain. Delicate. Tiny. If she looked anything like her mother, it was no wonder that Jake Dulan had fallen in love with the woman. He remembered Jake telling the stories of his many wives and how lovely they all were. At the time Tavish thought he was telling tall tales. After meeting three of his daughters, Tavish figured he wasn't stretching the truth any at all.

"Really, Uncle Tavish?" Merry said, wiping away the tears and letting him help her up on his big roan horse. "Did she ride when she was a little girl like me?"

"Of course she did, and when you get to California, I bet your new daddy gets you a horse and lets you ride too. Now you mustn't cry for Uncle Pat. He's not been home in a year. Been working on one wagon train or the other and he's ready to go back home and take care of his horses. Me, I'm going to work this job until we get to Echo Canyon, then I'm going home too. Meagan has probably grown a foot since I last saw her. I told her to stay just the way she was last year when I left, but you know these pretty lasses don't pay no attention to their uncle's advice."

"Well, one thing for sure, the man has the gift of gab. He didn't just kiss that Irish blarney stone, he's wallowed around on it for a lifetime," Gypsy muttered to her sisters as they began to walk beside the wagon.

"Still mad at him?" Garnet asked.

"He got me riled up last night and I didn't sleep so well," Gypsy said. "Yes, I'm still mad at him. I might stay riled at him until he leaves us at Echo Canyon. Thank goodness the fool isn't going all the way to California with us. He had no right to call me a squaw in that tone. Like I was dirt under his feet."

"Sometimes first impressions aren't really good," Gussie said.

"Sometimes they are the purest gospel in the book," Gypsy snorted.

"He is pretty short, but you two look kinda cute standing over there close together with little Merry Briley. And let me tell you something, little sister, it can get worse. You thought Pat O'Leary was a bag of wind at first but you kinda got to liking him here at the end," Garnet said.

"Don't even think thoughts like that, much less put them into words, about us looking cute together. If I'd wanted a short dark-haired man, they were a dime a dozen and wealthy to boot down in Texas. It would have made my grandparents happy. And yes, Tavish has taught me it can definitely get worse," Gypsy said coldly. "I'm about tired enough of all this journey. I'm thinking hard about catching a stage out of Fort Bridger when we get there next month and going back to south Texas."

"Thought you didn't leave anything there worth going

back to," Gussie said. "You agreed with the rest of us that you weren't welcome back there, just like none of us could go back to where we came from."

"Well, I think I can change my grandmother's mind," Gypsy said. "She was just angry and upset because I was going to see the fool who she blamed for stealing her own daughter out from under her nose, and then causing her to die. It was easier to blame Jake Dulan for her death than it was to just accept it. And then for me to announce I was going to see him on his sick bed. That really made her mad."

"But she died in childbirth. Our father couldn't have planned that," Garnet said. "Besides she was the only one who gave him the son he wanted, even if it did die with her."

"Yes, but grandmother said it was Jake's fault. He was too big of a man to be having children with my mother, Maria, who was even smaller than I am. So she hated him. Didn't your grandparents hate him too?" Gypsy asked.

"Of course. But mostly they hated him for leaving me behind," Gussie laughed. "I wasn't an easy child to raise up. That's why I got shifted from pillar to lamp post and almost put in an orphan's home a few times. Nobody wanted the offspring of that rakish Jake Dulan."

"You, Garnet?"

"I guess. I lived with an aunt here, a cousin there. Always a poor relative they took in for an extra set of working hands. Jake sure didn't do any of us any favors when he up and left us. Looks like he could've made room in his life for us even if our mothers were dead," Garnet said. "But that's water under the bridge. You're not really going to forsake us and go back to Texas. Lord, girl, when we get to Fort Bridger, we'll have more than half this trip done. It'll just be a downhill slide from there."

"Downhill to where? Right into the arms of some man I don't want to be married to," Gypsy said, looking back over her shoulder at the man bringing up the rear of the wagon train. *Like him. Someone who'll look down on me because my skin is a bit darker than everyone else's? Someone who'll be ashamed to have me walk down the street on his arm?*

## *Chapter Two*

"Okay, if everyone could be quiet," Hank, the wagon master, stood in the middle of the circle of more than 20 wagons and 100 women, plus one little girl. He raised his hand and the noise turned first into a soft buzz of whispers and then silence. A whippoorwill sang a lonely song in the distance and the oxen, already yoked together and hitched to the wagons, bawled in readiness, but the women were quiet.

Hank cleared his throat and pushed his spectacles up on his nose. "We'll be traveling without water the next four days. If all goes well, we'll hit the Sweetwater River then, and it'll stay with us for a long time. But for the next four days, we'll be going across some barren land. Your barrels are full. That's enough for drinking and cooking for each wagon. There'll be no bathing and for sure no washing clothes. We'll all be dusty and grimy, but once we reach the Sweetwater River, you can bathe and wash again. Any questions?"

No one said a word but the unspoken sighs could be felt all over the camp. Four days with no more water than what was in the barrel attached to their wagon. Gypsy dreaded every one of them. What she wouldn't give for a long, lazy bath back at the hacienda in Texas couldn't be measured in dollars and cents. It was her day to drive so she took her seat on the hard wagon seat, waited until the wagon train uncoiled from the night's rest and when it was her turn to pull out, she snapped the whip against the oxen's flanks.

The first day began.

She wondered if the gypsies had left the Rio Valley in south Texas by now. Paqui and her family had just arrived to help with the summer chores when Gypsy made her decision to go to St. Joseph, Missouri to meet her father, Jake Dulan. Abulita didn't like for Gypsy to spend time on the banks of the river where the gypsies camped every year, but she'd waited until her grandmother was asleep that last night before she was leaving the next morning and slipped away into the dark to visit with Paqui. The wrinkled old woman with her bright colored skirts and jangling bracelets read Gypsy's fortune under the stars that night. She told her that she'd have an adventure but there would be sadness at the end of it. But not to worry because there would be another adventure with enough happiness at the end to take away the sadness.

"Is there a tall blond-haired man in my adventure?" Gypsy had teased.

"There is a man in both adventures. One will not tell you what you want to know. The other, you will not want what he will tell you. You are a grown woman now, Gypsy Rose. You must learn to listen to your heart, my child, and study the stars. You'll find their secret if you are quiet and look inside yourself as you sit beneath the beauty of the stars," Paqui said, holding Gypsy's young hand in her own gnarled one and tracing the lines with a bent forefinger. "Your mother would be happy you are having these adventures. She would have liked to have adventures but it was not in her stars. If Jake Dulan had asked her to go away with him, she would have gone, but the end would have been the same."

"What was she like, Paqui?" Gypsy had asked.

"You. She was just like you. Only with brown eyes and not as much spunk. She used to sneak off in the moonlight to see me too. Your grandparents did not like her choice of husband but she was stubborn enough to listen to her heart," Paqui had smiled.

"Am I that stubborn?" Gypsy asked.

*"A que si!"* The woman declared with a soft laugh. "Isn't it so!"

"Did you tell her fortune?" Gypsy had wanted to know.

"Of course. I told her she'd have a beautiful daughter and an angel for a son. That her husband would hold her in his heart forever for giving him a son," Paqui had told her.

"But Paqui, that's not the way it really happened. She died," Gypsy'd argued. "What is really going to happen to me? What are you hiding in a maze of words?"

"You just study the stars, my child. You are too bright for your own good," Paqui had laughed aloud, and shooed her back to the ranchhouse.

Gypsy frowned at the memory. She'd had one adventure, riding that horrible stagecoach up through Texas, Indian Territory and into Missouri. And sure enough the man at the end of the journey couldn't tell her one thing about himself. Other than a handwritten will that gave each girl a mere taste of her own place in his life. Then there was the adventure of the wagon train. But there'd been no man on it. One waiting at the end for sure, who was nothing more than a name in a hat right now. What had Paqui seen in her hand that she didn't tell? No doubt, she'd seen a short lifetime for her mother, Maria, but she hadn't told her that. What had the old gypsy woman held back when she looked into Gypsy's future?

"Mercy, you look like you could kill someone," Garnet said, shading her eyes with the back of her hand as she looked up at Gypsy from the ground. "You've been too quiet these past two days."

"She's probably been polishing up that *bodkin* so she

could slit some poor Irishman's throat with it," Tavish said, riding by close enough to catch the bit of conversation.

"What are you talking about?" Garnet asked.

"That *bodkin* she carries in the folds of her skirt tail," Tavish said. "That dagger. You girls that share the wagon with her better be really careful. She could kill you in your sleep if you wiggle wrong and upset her."

"What's he talking about?" Garnet asked.

Gypsy shifted the reins to one hand and pulled a short-handled knife from her skirt. The sharpened metal gleamed when the sunlight struck it, and the carved wooden handle was a thing of great beauty; the head of a jet black stallion with his mane blowing back in the wind. "Didn't think it was any big thing. In my part of the country everyone carries a knife. Never know when a gun won't do the trick."

"Good grief," Gussie's blue eyes widened. "You been carrying that all along?"

"Sure. Carry it. Sleep with it. Use it when it's necessary. Just ain't been necessary. Came close to putting it between Rafe Pierce's shoulder blades when he rode off and left Willow standing there in all that misery, but a vision of Paqui shaking her head at me kept it sheathed," Gypsy said.

"Paqui? You know Paqui?" Tavish asked. "The gypsy, Paqui? Old woman of the clan that roams from one place to place?"

"Yes, what do you know of Paqui?" Gypsy asked, suddenly jealous that Tavish might know the gypsy she thought belonged to her personally.

"She and her clan winter in our area. They help my family with the horses. Fine horsemen. Help train the new stock every year. Paqui is the queen mother of the whole bunch. She tells them when it's time to go," he said, giving the bare essentials and not telling Gypsy the whole story.

"That's the truth," Gypsy said.

"She ever tell your fortune?" Tavish asked.

"That's none of your business, little boy," Gypsy said, sheathing her knife and ignoring him. So that's where the gypsies went when they left Texas in the fall. They worked their way back up to Utah Territory to winter with the Irish people. It was a small world after all. Paqui, no doubt, knew Tavish O'Leary as a small child, just like she did Gypsy.

*No she did not!* Gypsy thought. *It wasn't her Paqui. Paqui was as common of a name in the gypsies as Maria was amongst the Mexicans. So there, Tavish O'Leary, just ride your big chestnut-red horse on ahead and leave the back of the train alone.* She gripped the reins tighter.

On the second day without a river or creek close by, the women walked without talking. Gypsy recognized the signs and hoped they made it to the Sweetwater before they got downright mean with each other. She thought about the real desert they'd have to cross from Nevada to California and wondered if the women would ever make it, and what kind of bedraggled messes they'd be when it came time to present them to the husbands-in-waiting. Would there be water to wash with before their names went into the hat for the gold miners to pick amongst? Or would they be lined up with dirty faces and dusty skirt tails, calluses on their hands, and weariness etched in their faces?

"So what are you thinking about today?" Gussie asked.

"About the end of this adventure," Gypsy said, ignoring Tavish, who rode close enough to eavesdrop. "Will we meet the husbands after crossing that big desert with all the dust in the world bedded down in our sweat? Or will there be a river and a day to make ourselves pretty?"

"There'd better be some water because I'm not putting my red dancing dress on until I've had a decent bath," Gussie said.

"Red dancing dress?" Tavish asked, his dark eyebrow raised halfway to heaven.

"Of course, I was a saloon dancer before I signed on with this train," Gussie said without a hint of a blush. "You got a problem with that?"

"No ma'am," Tavish shook his head. What could Hank be thinking about? Half Mexicans? Saloon dancers? Couldn't he find decent women?

"Oh, Tavish," Connie, the lady who occupied part of the space in the wagon ahead of the Dulan girls and Annie, yelled back at him. "I made enough bean patties for your lunch today. When we stop for nooning, you just come on over to our wagon and sit with me."

"Thank you so much," Tavish grinned. Maybe Connie was a proper lady who didn't dance in saloons.

Merry Briley rode on the seat with her adopted mother, Annie, that day, and Gypsy walked. Dust boiled up around her feet from the iron wagon wheels, the horses, the oxen. Nothing moved that didn't create a stir in the dirt. Add that fine dust to the sweat pouring down her cheeks, into her eyes, and down the insides of her legs, and she, along with every other woman had every right to be cranky. At least all of them but Connie, who'd just commandeered Tavish for nooning. Well, power to the woman. That might be just what he needed anyway. Connie, the whining, gossiping girl who'd tried her dead level best to come between Willow and Rafe. Connie, who'd about driven Annie crazy when she shared the wagon with her until Willow left, and the Dulan sisters invited her to move. Connie, who was six inches taller than Tavish, and nine years younger. Now wouldn't that be a match made in the front courts of Hades, itself? It was so ludicrous it was even funny.

So why wasn't Gypsy laughing?

On the third day, Garnet drove the team and Gypsy walked again. If she made it to the Sweetwater River she intended to soak for hours. She wondered if she would ever feel clean again. The mirage of a nice cool river tumbling over rocks was all that kept her putting one foot in front of the other. She remembered the parties on the Texas-Mexico border when they'd prepared for weeks and danced until dawn. The pretty dresses. The food. The abundance of water for bathing. Why did she ever leave it?

"So, Miss Gypsy Dulan, how did you ever come by a name like that anyway?" Tavish pulled in his horse and kept him at a slow walk right beside Gypsy.

"That is none of your business," she said, wasting her breath even answering him. At least he didn't have to walk with the dust flying up to fill his nostrils. Oh, no, he had a beautiful dark red horse to ride on, and probably Connie waiting to wash his pretty face with a cool rag dipped in her own portion of drinking water at the nooning that day.

"Hey, lady, I don't like you one bit better than you do me. I was just making conversation to pass the time. This is the toughest part we have to cross for a long time. It's not easy on any of us, least of all me. I came across it just before I reached the camp that night you tried to kill me. And now I have to turn right around and go back across the barren, dusty mess," he smarted right back at her.

"I didn't try to kill you. If I'd tried, you would be dead. I don't make mistakes," she said.

"Yes, ma'am," he said, ice dripping off his words even as sweat stung his nearly black eyes. His jaw muscles worked in anger as he dropped back to follow the last train from a distance. That Gypsy Dulan was a piece of work. Jake was lucky her mother had died when she was a year old if the woman was a thing like the daughter she produced. Poor old Jake would've been tied to a shrew for the rest of his life. Neither Gussie, nor Garnet, were as mean spirited as Gypsy. They'd laughed and visited with him over the past three days, making the days go faster. But not so with the lovely little Gypsy girl. She'd barely looked at him and when she did . . . whew! If looks could kill he'd fall off his horse and be dead before his head hit the ground. He bet she wouldn't even come to the Irish wake in his honor. She'd just kick the dirt in on his grave and say some kind of curse on his eternal soul while she did it.

"You ever going to forgive that man for calling you a squaw?" Gussie asked.

"Sure, when he gets down on his knees and begs me," Gypsy said.

Gussie threw back her head and laughed so hard she had to wipe the tears from her eyes. "You know," she said between hiccups, "you sound exactly like Willow did when I tried to talk to her about Rafe Pierce."

Gypsy shot her oldest sister—a real beauty with tawny hair and Dulan blue eyes, taller than the other girls—the meanest look she could conjure up from the pits of her soul. "Don't you even think things like that, Gussie. Rafe Pierce was besotted with Willow from the first time he laid eyes on her at our father's funeral. It was plain as the nose on his face. He just couldn't make himself like her."

"You mean love her?" Gussie said.

"No, I mean like her. He loved her from the beginning whether he wanted to admit it or not. He didn't like her though. She wasn't the woman he thought she should be. You know, all prissy tailed, dependent and feminine. Willow was herself, and he could take it that way or leave it. Turned out he decided to like her for herself," Gypsy said.

"Well, you sure called that right," Gussie said.

Gypsy smiled for the first time in several days. "Do you wonder about them? I keep thinking maybe we'll find Velvet waiting at Fort Bridger. There's coaches that go from there to Fort Laramie, isn't there?"

"Wouldn't know," Gussie said. "I just hope she lived. She'll get in touch with us somehow if she did. If not along the way, maybe we'll have a letter waiting when we get to Bryte."

"I hope so," Gypsy said. *I hope you all hear from her and write me in Texas, because I can't take another minute of this boredom. Or of this dirty sweat rolling down my camisole or my toenails being dirty. I want a bath and I want to go back to where I'm someone. Not just a dark-skinned half-breed that white men, even Irishmen, turn their noses up at.*

## *Chapter Three*

Independence Rock loomed out ahead of the wagon train, beckoning to them, silently calling each of their names, reminding them that when they passed the bowl-shaped glacial remnant, they would have half the journey behind them. The Sweetwater River called to them even more, and Hank said they could stop in the middle of the afternoon to catch up on their laundry, refill their water barrels and have a bath. The closer they got to the big rock, the more Gypsy battled with her heart. She wanted to go home, and yet all her senses and emotions combined forces to tell her over and over she was making a bad decision if she did.

She trudged along with the rest of the women toward water and that strange shaped rock standing out there like a sentinel, waiting to tell them how strong they were for making it that far. Waiting for them to come and add their names to hundreds of others who'd gone on to the promised land before them. If she signed her name on that rock, then she'd have to go on to the end, or she'd be a traitor. It was the passing of one stage to another. To be strong enough to make it past the first half of the journey; to be strong enough to finish it. Put your name on the rock and draw from the strength it offered to keep going. A big old granite hill that had probably been standing there since the sixth day of creation. Gypsy eyed it with mixed emotions. Would she sign it? Would she go home to Texas?

They camped close to both the rock and the river. By the time Gussie got their wagon parked, the oxen unhitched and staked to feed on the green grass beside the river, laughter and splashing could be heard from the water. Gypsy began gathering her own dusty dirty clothing and bedding into a pile.

"Hey, let's go sign our names on the rock first," Annie said. "We're already dirty and dusty. If we take our baths and then go, we'll just be dirty again. So what do you say? Let's hike out there and get our name on the book saying that we're as big and mean as those first men who crossed this place."

"I vote yes," Garnet said. "I mixed us up some paint last night. It's in a bowl there in the wagon. I'm dying for a bath but when I get one, I sure do not intend to sweat again until tomorrow." She shaded her eyes from beneath a faded slat bonnet and looked up at the sky. "Sun won't be going down for a while yet. We've got time to get the laundry done and get it dry long before dark. Let's go sign our names, ladies. Miss Merry, you ready?"

"Yes, I am, but I want to change my name. Can I do it by signing it different?" Merry asked very seriously. "I want to change it to Wilson like Annie's. If she's going to be my mother, then I want to have her name, not Briley no more. You reckon it would be all right to sign my name as Merry Wilson on that rock?"

"Of course," Gypsy said. "It would be just fine. I think that would make it legal as it can be."

Tears welled up in Annie's eyes, but she wiped them away before anyone could see, and plastered on a smile. She sincerely hoped that when her name got chosen from the hat the man was as kind and sweet with Merry as Hank had been. Not all men would be willing to take on even a stepdaughter, let alone an orphan child. But if he didn't want Merry then Annie fully well intended to decline the marriage. No matter what kind of uproar it brought about.

"You aren't going to sign your name to that rock are you?" Tavish asked Gypsy. "Anyone coming along in the future will think some gypsy woman . . ."

"You can hush," Gypsy pointed her finger at him. "I'll sign it if I want to."

"But that means you plan on going the whole way to California and I heard you telling your sisters you didn't know if you wanted to go out there or not. Seems kinda crazy to me for you to keep on going anyway. Nobody is going to want a half breed with a temper. They'll throw your name back in the hat," Tavish said.

"That's enough." Gussie took two steps, stopping only when she was towering above him and looking down on the top of his black hair. "Gypsy is our sister and we'll hand her the knife and hold your sorry hide down for her to scalp you if you insult her again."

"Thanks, Gussie, but I can fight my own battles," Gypsy said. "And yes, Mr. O'Leary, I'm signing my name to the rock. And when we get to California, the man who gets my name, well, his gold mine will pale in comparison to what he has in me. You don't worry about those men not wanting a half breed. Not all of them are as mean as you are."

Tavish held up both hands and tipped his hat with one of them. "Accept my apologies, ladies." He waited until he mounted up to let the grin cover his face. He'd goaded her on purpose and gotten the desired results. She was a beauty when she was angry, and Tavish was sure enough a man to enjoy great beauty. Last night while he slept the memory surfaced in the form of a dream of Paqui telling him his fortune when he was a small child. He'd waited for many years to see if it would come true, and something stirring deep in his heart told him he was on the edge of finally seeing it.

No, he didn't like Gypsy Dulan one bit, but from the tales his father told about his mother, theirs hadn't been love at first sight either. So he needed a little more time to see if there was anything soft and nice about that youngest Dulan girl, and he'd gotten time by tormenting her. He still might have bitten off even more than an Irishman with the gift of gab could chew up, but at least he could make sure. It might still be, and most likely would be, that they'd go their separate ways when they reached the fork in the road where he planned to finish the last of his wagon train days. If they were still deciding on which one would hold the knife and which one would die when he reached Echo Canyon, he could always go home and forget her. If not, then perhaps Paqui had truly been blessed with the sight.

Garnet had prepared ahead of time, mixing axle grease and ashes into a nasty looking mixture to use to paint their names on the rocks with their fingertips. Gypsy stood aside and watched her and Gussie write their names beside each other: Augusta Beatrice Dulan, Garnet Diana Dulan. Merry Briley became Merry Wilson that day with her own scrawling penmanship, and Annie Wilson signed in for the rest of the journey. Aniece Bertha Wilson.

"Here," Gussie said, passing the bowl of homemade paint to Gypsy.

"No, thank you," Gypsy said as she took out her knife. If she was going to sign up for the long journey then she was doing it permanently. "You all go on back and get your baths. I'm going to be a little while."

"You really going to carve your name in that granite?" Garnet said. "Lord, girl, the paint will stay for years even with rain and snow."

"But will it be there in two hundred years? Will it be there when we are nothing but dust in the bottom of a six-foot hole? No, if I'm putting my name on this rock, it's staying forever," she said.

Garnet nodded. Gypsy had been fighting a multitude of demons the past few weeks. Ever since Velvet took sick, she'd not been the same happy-go-lucky little sister who'd take on a grizzly bear with a butter knife and determination.

If carving her name in that miniature mountain brought her a measure of peace, then Garnet wasn't going to argue with her about it.

"I'll gather up your dirty things and get them washed," Gussie said.

"I can do them later," Gypsy declared, choosing the spot right under her sister's names.

"Not if you're going to fight with that rock," Gussie said with a wave of her hand.

Gypsy didn't even see her wave, scarcely heard the humor in her voice. She'd already begun the first letter. The rock was tougher than she'd figured it would be, but it wasn't tougher than Gypsy Dulan. She painstakingly made a perfect M, followed it with an A, and then got lost in her thoughts as she worked, being very careful not to break the sharp tip from her dagger. A *bodkin,* that's what Tavish had called it. Must be Irish for a knife. She'd heard him refer to a small hill as a *torr,* and a loaf of bread as a *bannac*.

No doubt, she'd have a tough job sharpening her knife later that night, but she carried a small stone in her trunk that would put the blade back where it was useful again. She finished the A and started on the R. Time passed as she kept working and she didn't even see the storm clouds approaching from the southwest until a streak of lightning bounced off the rock in a great blue ball of energy and disappeared not far from her. Every hair on her head prickled, and she shivered when the thunder roared. She'd put the finishing touches on the last letter when the wind began to blow.

It was coming off hail for sure. The way its icy fingers reached through her clothing and chilled her rattled her bones left no doubt that there was hail in those big, low dark clouds with a green cast. One glance upward told her that she was going to get wet before she made it back to the wagons. A nervous giggle joined with the next clap of thunder. Four days they'd suffered dust and dirt, no water and heat, and now a storm was approaching, bringing water and coolness.

"Maria Marguerite Gypsy Rose Dulan," Tavish read aloud from right behind her. "And written in a fine hand with nothing but a *bodkin* to work with, I might add."

"What are you doing here?" she asked. "If you're going to put your name on the rock, you're going to have to do it in a hail storm."

"I'm not putting my name on that rock," Tavish said. "I'm not ever going to California. Chalk Creek, Utah is my home, and after this trip I'll have the money to buy the rest of a herd of horses I want. I already have a cabin and the land."

"I see," she said and turned to walk briskly back to the wagon train.

"Wait a minute," Tavish rode up beside her. "You'll never make it back before the hail hits, Gypsy. Ride with me."

"I'd rather be beaten to death by hail," she said.

"Probably," he laughed. "But Hank will have my hide if I don't bring you back safe. He sent me for you."

"Then he can have your hide," Gypsy kept walking.

Tavish leaned forward, whispered something in his horse's ear, and then let go of the reins. With two strong arms, he bent sideways and picked Gypsy up as if she were no bigger than Merry, and cradling her in his arms, gathered the reins back into his hands. "Now Maria Marguerite Gypsy Rose Dulan, we are going back to the wagons. Don't fight with me on this one. I'm not giving away my hide so easily."

Gypsy's heart pounded against her chest so hard she feared it would pop the buttons right off her dirty calico dress. Fear of her own feelings mixed with rage of losing a battle with Tavish O'Leary, combined with a warm feeling in the pits of her stomach, created an emotional upheaval that just plain bewildered Gypsy.

"So Maria was your christening name, Marguerite, your

confirmation name, and Gypsy Rose, the birth name your mother gave you. Why didn't she just name you Paqui if she liked the gypsies that much?" he asked around the hoarseness in his throat. Who would have thought she would fit so well in his arms? That her heart beating in unison with his would bring about such crazy, mixed-up feelings and desires in his heart? Was this what Paqui was talking about?

"Any good Catholic could figure that out in a minute," she said, but she didn't throw her head back and look up at him. She didn't need to look at him to see his mocking, dark eyes.

"And the Gypsy?" he asked, kneeing his horse into a fast trot. The first raindrops had already begun to fall and they were cold.

"Momma loved the gypsies and she'd always said she'd name her first child after them. Paqui was her favorite of course, but she said that just the sound of the word, Gypsy, made her smile. At least that's what she told Paqui, who told me. My grandmother hated the name. She called me little Maria most of the time."

"I like Gypsy just fine," Tavish said.

As if she cared what he liked, she told herself as dollar sized raindrops peppered down on her head from the dark clouds. Before long, pure mud would be streaming down her face when the water mixed with the dust of four days accumulation sticking to her black hair. She would have a bath in the river as soon as the lightning stopped, she promised herself. Until then, Tavish wouldn't look a bit better or smell better than she did.

Hail stones the size of ripe cherries sliced through the clouds and pounded their wet skin just as they reached the wagon train. Women were squealing and diving for cover. The hail was like gunfire as it hammered down against the wooden parts of the wagon, and bounced off the canvas covers like kids playing in a hayloft. In the melee, Tavish set her down on solid ground, tethered his horse to the back of her wagon and dived into the dry safety of the wagon right behind her.

"Hope you ladies have room for an extra body," he said, wiggling down in the small space between the corner of the wagon and Gypsy.

"History doth repeat itself," Gussie quipped, a twinkle in her eyes as she brushed out her long locks. She'd barely had time to gather the almost-dry clothes from the line before the first rain fell. It was in a pile in the middle of the wagon, gathering wrinkles by the minute. She just hoped the storm passed over quickly and the sun would come back out to finish the drying job, or else they'd have to contend with mildew.

"Hush!" Gypsy snorted, wiping the grime from her face. She didn't have to be told what her sister was thinking. There was a time when they first started out on the journey that Rafe Pierce had to seek refuge in their wagon. And now here was Tavish O'Leary pressed up against her tighter than a man had a right to be.

"Uncle Tavish, tell me a story," Merry begged. Her hair fell in ringlets around her face and down her back. A faded blue-checked dress the same color as her eyes was hiked up and showed the hem of her lace edged drawers.

"Well," he wiggled even closer to Gypsy, drawing warmth from the heat of her anger at him. But that could change someday, if he was patient and Paqui had really been kissed with the gift of seeing into the future. "Once upon a time," he said.

Gypsy rolled her eyes and got ready for a fairytale with an Irish touch. Tavish chuckled, and that raised her hackles even further.

"Once upon a time a band of gypsies came into an area. They had a beautiful little girl named Paqui who visited with the Irish fairies. Now these fairies are really just good folk who live in the forest. They don't have wings like you think of fairies, but they're quite small, little people who are very wise. So one day Paqui ran away from home because she was tired of traveling with the gypsies, and wanted to have a real home with a real porch and real flowers all around the house. Her parents were very sad and couldn't find her because you see the good folk had changed her into a very small little girl. They let her stay in their real little house inside the hollowed out log of an old dead oak tree for a little while but then told her that she must go back to her family. To cause them grief would make her heart hard. But they gave her a gift. Forever more she would be able to see the future and tell a person what to expect.

"So Paqui went back to her people and she travels to this day, telling people about their future and helping them to understand their past. Most years she comes to my part of the country in the winter time and I go and see her. When I was a little boy, no older than you are, she told me my future and I thought she was being very silly. But now that I am older, I think maybe the fairies did give her a gift."

"Is that a fairytale like Cinderella?" Merry asked.

"Of course it is," Gussie said. "Gypsies and little bitty people who live in hollow logs. There are gypsies in the world, Merry, and they are a lively bunch of people. They live by their own rules which are different than ours, but come on Tavish. Fairies?"

"Of course, it's only if you've been kissed by the Irish fairies and given freckles across your nose, that you would understand, me wee lass," he spoke with a heavy Irish brogue. His eyes glistened with merriment.

"I'm not sure I understand," Merry said. "Even if the Irish fairies did kiss me in my sleep. I'm not so sure I believe in someone seeing the future."

Garnet laughed out loud. "Now there's a child after my own heart. I think Merry is much more like I was at that age than like you, Tavish. I wanted real proof of everything. Still do. Forget all that stuff that comes out of the heart. I wanted to see it or touch it or else I sure didn't believe it. And love, along with fairies, is something untouchable, unseeable and I'm not so sure I believe in any of it."

"Oh, don't say that Garnet, love," Tavish thickened his brogue to sound like his grandfather. "Don't be temptin' the fates, me darlin' girl. 'Tis a wonderful day when a lass awakes to realize her own heart has fallen in love."

Garnet shook her head, her lips curving upward in a smile of disbelief. The little Irishman couldn't even charm a child completely. Neither could he convince her that the realities of life weren't cruel and cold. Gussie declared she'd tell the next story and went on with a very familiar one about a princess who lived in the woods. Gypsy sat quietly in her corner, wedged tightly between a trunk and Tavish O'Leary, a cold chill tickling her backbone, in spite of the warmth generated by a well-muscled male body right next to her.

Later that night, she lay against the back of the wagon and thought again of the story he told. Gussie and Garnet were sleeping soundly in their freshly washed bedding; Annie snored so slightly it was more like the purr of a contented momma cat with Merry curled up tightly around her back. They'd all be outside in their bedrolls if the ground wasn't soaked. There had been few nights in the journey that they'd had to sleep inside the wagon, crammed into the small space like little piglets, but Gypsy didn't mind that night. Her mind was too busy trying to make some kind of sense of the past few days to worry about her toes touching her sister's bare feet. Gypsy raised the wagon sheet and looked out at the stars. It was hard to believe that not five hours before dark, clouds covered the sky and rained hail down upon them for half an hour. Now the moon hung in the sky and the stars twinkled around it, like the little fairies Tavish told about.

Had her Paqui really told his fortune? Or was he just teasing and making up something to entertain Merry? If she had read his palm what had she seen there? What was the secret she kept talking about up there in the stars?

Questions upon questions. And all Gypsy Rose Dulan could do was wait for the answers because they sure weren't hers to have that night. She breathed in the night air and caught a whiff of something else. It was Tavish or at least his scent. Lye soap, some kind of scented water he used on his face after he shaved, the masculine smell of a man after a hard day's work. She raised the sheet and peeped out. No one was there. The whole train was quiet, with only the occasional whining of a horse or oxen. A cricket and a locust vied for center spot in one of nature's operas off in the distance. But Tavish O'Leary wasn't standing right outside the wagon letting the wind waft his scent into her snug sleeping quarters.

Then she realized where the scent came from. He'd been crammed into the corner and the wooden wagon bed had picked up his scent. She rolled her eyes and turned her back to the boards. That's all she needed—to be reminded of the bane of her heart while she tried to fall asleep. But every breath brought back the story he told and the way it rang true in her heart when she'd listened.

It was the same story Paqui had told her when she was a little girl. Even if she didn't believe there were Irish fairies or good folks who lived in tree logs, she did believe the same Paqui had known both Tavish and Gypsy as small children. Not that that bit of information made a single difference in anything.

However, she was still mulling it over in her mind when sleep finally came, only to bring her dreams of the gypsies and their wagons coming into south Texas for another summer. Only this time there was a small dark-haired boy with them, and he stood staring down at a little baby girl still in a cradle, vowing that he would protect her forever.

She awoke at dawn in a cold sweat, glad that the sun was rising, chasing the darkness of the night and the silly dream from her mind. All that talk about fairies and gypsies had created the dream, she was sure. Daylight would bring another hard day on the trail and reality back into her life. Like Garnet said, if Gypsy couldn't touch it, see it, or feel it with her fingertips, she darn sure wasn't about to believe in it.

## *Chapter Four*

Tavish's thin shirt didn't provide much padding against the rough bark of the ancient oak tree, but he leaned against it anyway, resting his arm on a rock. It made for a right comfortable chair if he didn't think about the comforts waiting inside his cabin back at Chalk Creek. A real bed stuffed with feathers his mother and sisters had harvested for two years during fryer killing season. Pillows, as soft as the clouds up there in the sky. Two big rocking chairs his grandfather had crafted with his own hands with bright colored pillows in the seats. Homesickness penetrated every nerve in his body. He was ready to go back and settle down. With a wife. Old Paqui had said he'd meet a blue-eyed beauty and he had, but it was as evident as the blarney in an Irishman's heart that he hadn't met the right one yet. For a while there he'd entertained notions about Gypsy Dulan, but the past two days, since they'd passed the Independence Rock, she'd not spoken a word to him. Not even a hateful one.

He stretched his short frame to force out the cramps of a hard day's ride. A few dark clouds skittered across the sun, trying hard to go to bed for the night on the western horizon. Nothing more than a sliver of pale yellow light saying goodnight, and leaving the rest of the evening up to the moon. Tomorrow they'd reach South Pass, another milestone on the journey. Before too many weeks, he'd have his part of the job done. Someone else would take his place and he'd go home.

His wide mouth curved upward into a bright smile when he thought of home. Chalk Creek, Utah. The closest thing to Clare, Ireland his grandfather could find, he'd said often enough. Not that Tavish thought for a minute that the harsh winters and unforgiving summers in Utah could be anything like the misty mornings on the green, green grass of Ireland. His grandmother had told him about the lovely Ireland, and someday he fully well intended to go have a look for himself.

Lying there on his back, the sun resting after a hard day's work, the stars not yet visible, Tavish finally realized what his grandfather had found when he looked at north central Utah. It wasn't a physical place like his old home in Ireland, but it had a heart full of love with Tavish's grandmother and their extended family. That's what made the place as beautiful as his beloved Ireland. Tavish sighed, wondering if he'd ever find that same thing deep within his own Irish heart.

Gypsy slipped away from the camp and wandered slowly toward the river. She'd never craved quietness so much in her life. She'd been raised in a home booming with family. Her mother, the youngest of a family of eight children, had been the only one to die young so there were lots of cousins and uncles and aunts, all of whom lived somewhere on the ranch. But in the midst of all that noise, she'd had a room she could sneak off to or a stable she could run to.

Nowadays, during the daytime, she walked with her sisters, Gussie and Garnet, or with their other wagon mates, Annie and Merry, or some of the other women who might straggle back to visit during the day. At nooning the women congregated in great groups to eat and talk about the weather, the difficulty of the journey, the husbands awaiting at the end. In the evening, it was more of the same as they unhitched the oxen, prepared the evening meal and prepared for the next day. Seldom did she find a moment of solitude, and Gypsy's low spirit was in desperate need of a few minutes of pure, plain quiet.

Without a sound, she made her way through the sage brush toward the river. She imagined the cool water on her feet and the sound of the crickets and toad frogs singing in the warm night air. Too bad she wouldn't hear the howl of a lonesome coyote. That kind of noise she could appreciate. Not the constant sound of women's worries about their future husbands.

She yearned for her home in Texas. Thought of the big feather bed in her room, covered with brightly embroidered quilts and pillows; the soft cushions in the chair beside the window where she could look out over the flat land, all the way to where the sun came up in the morning and went down in the evening. Gypsy admitted she was so homesick she could cry for it, but there was no going back now. She'd go forward with her life and hope when she reached Bryte, California, there would be a hundred women still living, and she wouldn't have to marry a man she didn't know, much less love. She wanted a love like her mother had for Jake Dulan. One that would defy everything even if it was shortlived. She wondered if Jake had really loved her mother as much as she'd loved him?

The soft sound of the river and the coolness on her bare feet soothed her heart and soul. She leaned back in the tall, soft green grass and let her gaze go again to the sky. The stars would be peeking out soon. Would they ever give up their secrets like Paqui had said? *No, they wouldn't,* she thought. *Because the secret isn't up there in the stars after all. It's not the stars that give up their secrets. It's the fact that to study them you have to get alone in the quietness and it's there in silence that you find the real secret. That's what's deep in your own heart. That's why Paqui said to study them and they'd reveal the secrets. But what's in my heart?*

Breaking her thoughts about her newly found revelation, a lonesome whispered song floated on the warm night breezes to Gypsy. A haunting melody in a rich tenor voice, sang partly in English about a young girl who carried a banner of white, orange and green, and partly in Irish that she couldn't understand. Patrick O'Leary had sang some of the same melody to Merry when she rode with him.

Gypsy rolled her eyes toward the dusky skies. Tavish O'Leary had no right to interfere with her quiet. She'd waited all day for the evening so she could spend some time alone. She jerked her feet from the water in anger, pulled on her socks and boots and stomped back toward the camp.

"Who goes there?" The singing stopped and Tavish's accented voice cut through the air.

She ignored it.

"I said who goes there?" he asked again. "Oh, 'tis but you, Gypsy Rose Dulan. You can't hide that black hair even in the twilight of the evening."

"What are you doing here?" she asked.

"I'm searching for peace and quiet. The women, they are a wonderful lot. But me heart seeks some solitude to ponder. 'Tis a lovely evening. Come and join me. We can sit here and think upon the stars where the river flows on toward the great ocean. We don't have to talk. Me heart is not in the idea of visiting right now. Just in sitting in the calm night that the good Lord made."

"An Irishman not wanting to talk? That's a joke," Gypsy stopped. He'd been no more than 15 yards from her the whole time. Just up the river a piece, sitting with his back to a tree. She'd no doubt passed close earlier in the evening but he'd either ignored her or been so deep in his own thoughts he hadn't heard her.

"Might be, but me heart is not in the words tonight, just

in the feeling of the peace," he said. "Come and share the tree with me. I'll not bite, I promise."

She stood no more than six feet from the tree, and by the light of the moon she could see the viper winding its way down the tree. It was barely six inches from Tavish O'Leary's fine black hair when it stopped, drew back its head and prepared to strike.

"Sit very still Tavish. Don't move a muscle. Don't talk and don't move. I mean it," she said.

Tavish chuckled. "Don't be tryin' to scare me, Gypsy Rose. 'Tis a fine night and if you don't want to sit with me, then just say so. I won't chase you down the river. I'm just offering you some space to think quietly away from the buzz of the camp."

"I said don't talk," she whispered.

"But—"

One moment he was filling his eyes with her fine figure, the next he saw the flash of the blade and knew he was a dead man. All because he hadn't hushed when she told him to do so. That was no way for a good Irishman to leave the world. Killed by a blue-eyed beauty because he couldn't do the impossible and keep his mouth shut.

In three easy strides she was beside him, had removed the dagger from the tree right above his right ear and threw it with a violent thrust to the ground. The snake, minus a head, fell on the stone where his hand lay. He jumped, shaking his arm as if dislocating it from his shoulder would erase the feel of the serpent from his skin.

Gypsy kicked the still wiggling remains of an eight-foot bull snake away from the rock. "You eat snake?" she asked.

"Never been that hungry, yet," he said, wiping the remnants of the vile thing from his bare arm.

"Me, neither," she said, pulling her knife from the ground and putting it back in the folds of her well-worn, faded blue skirt.

"Guess that's one thing we can agree on," he said, his voice deeper than it had been when he was singing the Irish song. "I'll walk with you back to the campsite. Guess I owe you me life now."

"No, thanks, I can walk by myself. And I don't want your life. You can keep it. I just didn't want the snake to strike you. Could've made you sick. Don't have time to contend with a sick man," she said.

Before he could shoot off a snide remark, a dozen Indians on horseback appeared like ghosts out of the twilight. Gypsy fingered the knife and Tavish wished for his gun which was back at the men's campsite. They weren't wearing war paint and they all were smiling, so maybe they weren't going to raid the camp with two black scalps already hanging from their coup belts.

The Indian riding in front held out his open palm. His face was the same color as Gypsy's boots and appeared to be made of the same fabric. Down in the wrinkles were glittering, dark eyes under heavy, bushy eyebrows. His black hair, iced with silver streaks, hung past his shoulders and even with the hand up, he looked ferocious to Gypsy.

"Hello," Tavish said in what he hoped was the right language, and held up a hand. He knew only a smattering of one Indian tongue, the one that he'd learned from his friend, Buffalo Boy, when he was a little boy.

The Indian shook his head.

*Wrong one*, Tavish thought.

Bobby, the Indian guide for the wagon train, stepped out of the shadows and said something in a few calm words to the Indians. "This is Dancing Bear," he told Tavish and Gypsy. "He sent word last week he would come and trade with us before we got to South Pass."

Bobby said a few more words to the Indians, and Dancing Bear nodded, saying a few words back to Bobby, who motioned for them to follow him back to camp. The Indian sat still on his horse and stared intently at Gypsy, then spoke fast and furious.

Bobby chuckled and began to refuse his offer.

"What does he want?"

Before Bobby could answer, a feminine giggle came out of the darkness. “Oh, Tavish O’Leary, I know you are out here because I saw you leave the camp a while ago. Tell me where you are so I can find you.”

*Connie!* Gypsy shook her head. So the wagon train’s biggest flirt had set her cap for Tavish O’Leary. Well, she’d set it for Rafe Pierce, too, but he had fallen in love with Willow. If Tavish knew what was good for him, he’d saddle up that big red horse and light a shuck for Utah without looking back. Connie would plague him until he either succumbed to her flirtations, he dropped down stone cold dead, or rode off to get away from her. The first choice would bring a lifetime of misery; the second, an eternity of misery because Gypsy had no doubt Tavish O’Leary would be weaving his blarney a long time before he talked himself past the front gates of heaven; the last, well, he’d better ride hard and fast, and hide deep in a forest if he wanted to get away from Connie.

Connie didn’t even see the Indians until she was right on top of them, then screamed and fell against Tavish’s chest. “Oh, save me,” she wailed. “Don’t let them scalp me. Give them Gypsy instead. She’s like them. They’ll think she’s just another squaw.”

The sight of the woman trying to coax sympathy out of Tavish was enough to make Gypsy giggle. “Oh, Connie, go on back to your wagon,” Gypsy said. “You’re just high strung and always looking for attention. These Indians are here to trade with Hank not haul you off to be a slave in their tribe. Tomorrow night we’ll have buffalo to go in our stewpot,”

“Tavish, take me back to the wagons?” she whimpered.

“I think you can find your own way back,” Tavish said as he unwrapped her arms from around his neck and dropped them to her side. She might be a beauty and she might have blue eyes, but he wasn’t encouraging one moment of flirtation with that woman. She was a gossiping shrew that could lose him his job as well as the money for the horses he needed to start his own operation. And it hadn't taken a revelation from heaven itself to tell him so, either.

"But I'm scared. What if they attack me when my back is turned?" Connie whined.

Gypsy took her by the arm and led her a few feet back toward the wagons. "Go on back to your wagon before you lose the rest of your dignity. The supply is getting mighty slim, girl. And you rely upon it and your ego to carry you through most days. Someday, when you grow up, you'll trade them in for a backbone, but until you do you better guard them with your life because they're all you got," Gypsy whispered so low no one else could hear.

"You are nothing but a half-breed Mexican, and no man will ever want you," Connie shouted, slinging her nose into the air and prancing back to the wagons with a prissy step the Queen of England couldn't have found a single fault with.

Bobby laughed out loud and Gypsy whipped around to shoot him a look that would have dropped a grizzly bear in its tracks. "What's so funny?" she asked, icicles dripping off every word. "You think that's funny, what she said?"

"No ma'am," Bobby wiped his eyes. "Connie is just trouble walking. I pity the man who has to claim her for his wife. I'm not laughing at that at all. What is funny is that the chief here wants to know if we'd take two dressed buffalo for you. He says he likes your blue eyes and he wants you for his son's first wife. He saw you throw your knife at a snake and kill it swiftly, then kick the wiggling varmint to the side. He says you have great courage and he would have you trained as a . . ." Bobby searched for the right word. "A shaman-type person. He says you have the gift of sight with those blue eyes and he would be honored to have you for a daughter."

For the first time in her life, Gypsy Rose Dulan was totally speechless.

"I told him you'd already been bought and paid for, that

we were just delivering you and all these women to your husbands in California," Bobby said.

The chief mumbled something Gypsy didn't understand but the language was soft and beautiful. Maybe she should tell Bobby to tell them to bring on the buffalo and she'd go willingly with the chief. Surely she'd be revered in the camp since she had blue eyes. Even Tavish thought she was an Indian squaw so she ought to fit right in with them.

"He says he'll make one more offer. Two horses of our choosing. Think I ought to take the offer to Hank?" Bobby grinned impishly.

"Take what?" Hank said. "Hello, Dancing Bear. What's going on with Connie? I saw her sneaking out of camp and followed her. That girl can get into more trouble than a sane wagon master can keep up with."

"Two horses and two whole buffalo for the woman with the blue eyes and enough courage to kill the big snake," Dancing Bear stated his price.

"No, can't do it, but we'll trade for some buffalo. How about tobacco and sugar?" Hank said.

"Whiskey?" Dancing Bear asked.

"No, not carrying any of that. This is a different wagon train. We're taking these women to their husbands who have already bought them," Hank told him.

"Tell him I'll give him my knife," Gypsy said, pulling the dagger from the folds of her skirt, the moonlight glittering on the sharp blade. "Tell him if he'll steal Connie, I'll give him the knife and everything in my trunk. Clothes, handmade boots. All of it. She's got blue eyes and corn silk-colored hair. His son would be proud to have her."

Bobby's eyes twinkled as he relayed the message.

"He says that your knife is a thing of great beauty but his son would use it on him if he took that screaming banshee back to his tribe," Bobby said.

"Well, some days start out bad and then get worse," Gypsy said. "I'm going back to camp and getting a good night's sleep. Tomorrow might be better. Maybe the next bunch of Indians will take my knife and Connie with it."

"He says he'll up it to five horses," Bobby yelled at her back. "Hank is considering."

"Drop dead. If he wants a woman he can have Connie," Gypsy threw over her shoulder as she sheathed her knife. Her full, sensuous mouth broke into a wide smile as she stomped back toward the camp. He might be an Indian chief, but by golly there was one man out there who saw some worth in a half-Mexican woman with Dulan blue eyes.

"Wait a minute," Tavish said right behind her. "They can do the trading without me and I asked if you'd like to sit in the darkness and soak up some peace and quiet."

"I can't afford anymore peace and quiet," she stopped, the stars meeting flat ground behind her, the glow of campfires in front of her. "It's already scared ten years off my life. I hate snakes. Really hate them. Before I can get the nasty touch of one off my knife, I look up and there's Indians appearing like ghosts. Connie yelling at me. I think there's more peace and quiet in the wagon train than beside the river."

"Maybe tomorrow night?" Tavish asked.

"Why?" Gypsy raised a perfectly arched eyebrow at him.

"I don't know, Gypsy Rose. I just feel a need in me heart to know you."

"You might not like me."

"I already don't like you. But there might be something there I'm overlooking. Tomorrow night?"

"We'll see." She turned quickly away from his handsome face and muscular bare arms.

One second she was going to the camp. The next he'd twirled her around and she was in his arms, his lips on hers. Goosebumps the size of the hill in Ash Hollow raised up on her arms; every hair on her neck tingled with excitement; a low knot of pain tightened up deep in her belly. Stars exploded around her like dynamite.

"Take that to bed with you and see if you have any peace and quiet tonight," Tavish said in a hoarse whisper.

He was 20 feet from her and humming that haunting Irish song when she came to her senses. For the second time in one night the normally very loquacious Gypsy Rose was struck silent.

## *Chapter Five*

Tavish kissed Mary Ellen O'Brian when he was 14-years-old out behind the barn at one of his cousin's weddings. He'd made a habit of kissing whenever opportunity arose ever since then, but nothing had ever prepared him for the restlessness in his heart after he shared that impulsive kiss with Gypsy Rose Dulan. The next day he kept his distance, riding far enough back that he couldn't hear the constant chatter of the women; close enough that he could see her every move.

When she pushed her bonnet back and rotated her neck, he wished he could rub away the aches of the day's journey. When she removed a handkerchief from her sleeve and mopped the sweat from under her nose, he envisioned bathing her face in the cool water of the stream running through his land. At nooning, he and Hank had lunch with the Dulan ladies and Annie. Both he and Gypsy were careful not to look at each other, replacing thorny barbs and hateful looks with an awkward silence.

Gypsy was nigh on to 20-years-old and she'd long since ceased believing in the foolishness that fed teenage girls' fantasies. Swooning when a man merely looked your way. The world standing still when he kissed you. All that was the fodder of summer afternoon naps between the barbecue for dinner and the dances after supper. It certainly wasn't something that really happened, and to prove it she served Tavish his lunch herself, being very careful not to let her fingers brush against his or to look into his eyes. That point proven, she rationalized that it had been the power of the moment she'd felt. First the snake, which she hated. Then the Indians and the surge of fear filling her breast when she first saw them. Add Connie to that already crazy, mixed-up mixture, with her whining and cajoling, and then the offer from the chief to buy Gypsy. It was certainly enough to electrify every sense in her small body.

No doubt, Tavish would have had the same rush of emotions bouncing through him. After all, the snake had actually touched his skin. The kiss was an impulsive action and should be treated as such. It would never happen again. She'd see to that for sure. Tavish wasn't ugly, not by any means, but he most certainly was not the man for her. Not with those dark, brooding looks.

Hank called the nooning finished in about 30 minutes. Garnet rubbed the numbness from her backside, not even caring that Tavish O'Leary watched. Riding on that wagon seat might relieve the aching feet she had when it was her days to walk, but it didn't do a thing for her fanny.

"What?" she asked when Gypsy gave her a dirty look. "Just because you wouldn't touch your posterior in front of your Irish honey, doesn't mean I can't."

"He's not my honey," Gypsy said, coldly. "It's just that we need to maintain some kind of . . ." she stammered looking for the right words.

"Some kind of protocol," Annie finished for her as they took up the afternoon's journey toward South Pass. "What she's saying is that just because we are all women on the wagon train, we still need to have some kind of modesty. It wouldn't do for us to get to California acting like hoydens."

"Well, pardoooon me," Garnet wiggled her head and laughed. "My fanny is numb from riding. It doesn't know anything about protocol. What we all need is nice plump cushions to ride on. I'm afraid my petticoats and drawers don't give me nearly enough padding."

"It'll toughen us up," Gussie said. "I need lots more toughness to marry a man I've never even met. By the time we all reach Bryte, California, we'll be tough enough that those men better not even blink an eye at marryin' us. When we get there I'm getting my dancing dress out and marching right down the main street in it."

"You'll be tough and beautiful both," Annie said.

"You bet I will, and any man who thinks he can tame Gussie Dulan better think again."

Gypsy listened with one ear and wished Tavish wasn't riding behind her. Was he thinking about that kiss? Probably not. He was a man, and men didn't think about things like that. They just took what they could and rode away. Jake Dulan had certainly proven that point well enough.

Tavish was so engrossed in watching Gypsy he didn't hear two wagons bearing down upon them until a whiff of dust filled his nostrils, making him yank his bandanna back up to cover the lower half of his face. Two men rode on the seat of each of the Conestoga freight wagons pulled by 12 oxen. Four others rode horseback with them. Eight in all, yelling and flapping their hats at the women as they passed. Some of the women waved back; some ignored them.

Gypsy was of the latter.

The day wore on. Gypsy couldn't keep her thoughts off Tavish. He suffered from the same malady. At the end of the day when Hank told them to circle up beside a wide spot on the river, both of them were edgy, touchy and in dire need of a quiet hour in complete solitude, with neither wanting to go outside the circle of their own camp for fear of finding the other already beside the river.

Annie cooked that night. Beans, seasoned with bacon grease leftover from breakfast. She saved back enough grease to fry up the last of their buffalo steaks, made a pan of biscuits and set them to cook over the top of the cast iron Dutch oven where the beans boiled. Garnet unhitched the oxen and staked them out to feed on what green grass could be found. Gussie rustled around in the wagon, digging in her trunk, fingering the red dancing dress lovingly, and dragging out her change of undergarments so she could have a bath while supper cooked. Merry went visiting amongst all the wagons like she did every night.

*Oh, to be a little girl again and not have to face the feelings and heartaches of adulthood,* Gypsy thought as she pulled her boots off and rubbed her tired feet. Tomorrow she would drive, and by nightfall she'd be wanting to do the same thing Garnet did earlier. Rub her fanny. Paqui had said she'd have two adventures. Seemed like an adventure should be a perfect piece of paradise. Not a boring, day-after-day walk toward something she wasn't even sure she would accept when she reached the end.

"Hank sent me to tell everyone to stay close to camp tonight. Those freight wagons might not be so far ahead of us after all, and he wouldn't want trouble," Tavish said right at her elbow.

Gypsy jumped, a tingle raising the hair on the back of her neck.

"What kind of trouble?" Annie raised up from a stooped position where she'd been checking the biscuits.

"You saw those men. Kinda rough and might be disrespectful if they caught a woman out alone," Tavish said.

"Hank knows best," Annie said. "When you run on to Merry, tell her to get back here to our camp. I'll keep her close."

"Hey, wait a minute, does that mean no baths or washing?" Gussie pulled back the wagon sheet and stuck her head out, her golden hair flowing past her shoulders, forming a halo around her beautiful face.

"It means, no one is to leave the camp alone. Just a precaution. If you ladies want a bath and to do a little washing, take two others with you. No party of less than three is to leave camp, and be sure to keep an eye on your neighbors. I'll tell Miss Merry to come on home," Tavish nodded toward Annie and went on his way, stopping at each of the circled up wagons. His swagger reinforced Gypsy's belief that he'd forgotten all about what had transpired between them the night before. He smiled at Connie when she threw the back of her hand across her forehead and rolled her eyes. Heaven help those men, Gypsy thought, if they hogtied the lovely fair-skinned Connie and drug her off to be their woman on the trip. She'd cut them to pieces with her sharp tongue before a one of them had time to lay a hand on her. Before an hour was up they'd be pleading with Hank to take everything in their wagons just to take her back.

"You coming along?" Gussie asked Garnet and Gypsy. "That would make the three of us. Wouldn't no mule skinner this side of St. Jo tackle all three of us at one time."

"Sure," Gypsy said. Three women would be better than more than a hundred. Even if it was just for a few minutes.

They shucked their clothes down to camisoles and drawers and waded out into the clear water, splashing it up on their sweaty arms and necks even before they were deep enough to really begin to bathe. They applied lye soap to every naked part, then cleansed their undergarments right on their bodies.

"Still going to chicken out on the husband business?" Gussie asked Garnet, who'd declared from day one that she was just along for the adventure and to get to know her sisters.

"Yep, I'm still going to. Way I see it is that a marriage would be a horrible thing if both parties already loved each other. That first year is held together with passion and love alone. To start out as perfect strangers with no love. Why, that'd be asking for a miracle, and I don't believe in miracles or Irish fairies." Garnet leaned back and washed the soap from brilliant red curly hair that fell to her waist.

"Why did you have to mention Irish fairies?" Gypsy moaned.

"That man is getting under your skin. Isn't he?" Gussie asked, doing the same with her long, blond hair that Garnet was. Washing the lye soap from it. She would have given anything for half a dozen eggs to give it a real treatment and make it glow.

"Yes, he is," Gypsy admitted honestly. No use lying to her sisters. They might not have known each other growing up but the same Dulan blood flowed in all their genes, and they were at least honest with each other. "But that don't mean a thing. One time I fell backwards into Abulita's, that's my grandmother's, rose bushes and thorns stuck in my skin. It hurt like the very devil but we pulled them all out, and in a week I didn't even remember the pain. Same with Tavish. It's not that it's romantic. Just the way he's always around with that Irish lilt to his voice. Besides he doesn't appeal to me."

"Oh, no?" Garnet said, wiping the stinging soap from her eyes. Just one time she'd like to wash her hair without getting soap in her eyes. It was the bane of curly hair, she determined years ago. All those curls bouncing around couldn't be tamed and they threw soap into her eyes.

"Shut your eyes," Gussie said.

"Which one of us?" Gypsy grinned.

"Both of you," Gussie said. "Garnet, you shut your eyes and the soap will shed off your eyelids. Gypsy, you shut your eyes, really, and keep them shut."

"Okay, is this a game? Is there a snake swimming near me?" Gypsy asked.

"No, it's not a game. Now keep them shut. Can you see me?"

"Of course not. That's a silly question," Gypsy said, keeping her eyes shut.

"If I was Tavish O'Leary this close to you, what would you feel?" Gussie asked.

Gypsy blushed but she was tongue tied. To answer a

question truthfully was one thing. To admit what lay deep in her heart was quite another.

"Think about it. Your heart doesn't know if a person is tall or short. If he's a Greek god or a dark-eyed Irishman. It just knows who it wants to make it whole. I'm not saying Tavish O'Leary is the man for you. Heaven forbid. I'm not so sure there'd be enough love in the Good Book to hold you two together for that first year Garnet mentioned. But what I'm saying is, don't get it set in your mind that you'll have only one type of man and let one get away who would treat you like a queen; who would be the one that your heart already recognizes who would make you a whole woman. Now open your eyes and get your hair washed. I bet Annie has supper ready and Merry was starving long before we stopped."

"Thanks, Gussie," Gypsy said. "I'll think on what you said."

"That's all I ask," Gussie said, finding a grassy spot to stand while she stripped out of her unmentionables and dried her body on a bath sheet. In moments she was re-dressed in clean drawers, camisole, petticoat and faded but clean blue-checked dress. When she reached California, she hoped to never see another faded dress in her life. She didn't mind wearing dresses from one year to the next, but everyday in the sun had bleached the colors from everything she owned. Except her red dancing dress.

Garnet and Gypsy followed suit and in a few minutes they were all traipsing back inside the camp. None of them saw the man standing behind the trees in the grove not far from where they bathed.

After supper, there was little visiting as the women bedded down for the night. Gypsy lay under the wagon on the outside, Merry next to her, curled up as usual next to Annie. Garnet and Gussie on beyond that. The things Gussie said out there in the river kept playing through her mind, like a song would do after a night of dancing. The only noises were women's snores and sighs. She couldn't hear a single cricket or tree frog. Nothing to ease the restlessness in her heart where Gussie's words were almost set to guitar music. Listen to your heart. Listen to your heart. It will never steer you wrong. What it all boiled down to was the same thing Paqui had said. Go out alone and study the stars to find their secrets. Shut your eyes and listen to your heart in the quietness.

But what if she didn't like what her heart said?

The moon was high in the sky, the stars glistening around it like tiny little candles around a huge bonfire. She strained her ears, trying desperately to hear the river's water rushing along over stones and soft sand. Nothing. She couldn't drag up anything, not even when shc shut her eyes and begged her imagination to work overtime.

Everything was quiet out there; noisy with sleep inside the camp. Surely, the mule skinners on their two freight wagons would be sound asleep by now, she reasoned. And there would be no sleep for her if she didn't have a few moments of solitude. She'd just lie there, tossing from one side to the other, worrying about the future, condemning the past until the first little rays of sun broke through the night to start another day.

She eased out from under the wagon, pulled the sheet she'd used as cover around her night rail and took two steps out into the darkness. Just a little way, she told herself as she stopped and listened. Just far enough she couldn't see the women, hear their night noises; just far enough to hear the water and nature's night noises. Not all the way to the river. Only a little further. She took three more steps. A cricket sang its melancholy song out there in the distance and she smiled. Two more steps. A tree frog added his rich bass voice, making a duet. One more step. Could that really be a coyote, finishing out the ensemble? She stifled a giggle.

A prickling sensation chased chills down her spine. Drat that Tavish O'Leary! He was supposed to be asleep in his little camp, not out here in the darkness with her. Couldn't she have a moment's peace without him disturbing it? She turned to give him a healthy dose of her mind and looked up into the evil eyes of a man who was at least six-feet tall and the size of a full-grown, longhorn steer. Instinctively, she reached for her knife in the folds of her night rail—but it was under her pillow. She started to scream but a big, smelly beefy hand shot out and covered her mouth. Another wrapped itself around her, tucking her up under a sweaty man's arm, and carrying her hurriedly away like a bag of potatoes.

Tavish flipped from his right side to his left. He shut his eyes so tight in search of sleep that his head began to ache. He tried thinking of something other than Gypsy. Annie and Hank, for instance. Annie was besotted with Hank and he wouldn't be a bit surprised if when the time came for husband choosing in California that Annie refused anyone but Hank. Poor old Hank, 40-years-old, and never had a family, was about to get a wife and a child to boot. And it was going to blindside him. That brought on thoughts of the man who'd get Gypsy, and he was back to square one.

"Be still and go to sleep," Bobby complained for the third or fourth time. Tavish sighed loudly.

Tavish sat up and let his eyes fixate on the dying embers of the fire. Even in them a vision of Gypsy appeared. Finally, he eased away from the camp and went down to the edge of the river. Checking the tree he chose to lean against for any sign of another snake, he sat down and let his mind go where it would. Play out the scenes as it wanted, tire him out so he could sleep.

A faint squeak broke into his thoughts but he ignored it. Most likely a night owl who'd just sunk his claws into a field mouse. Rustling in the sage brush proved him to be right. The owl lost the mouse and was having to scramble to regain his supper. Tavish felt sorry for the old boy. Keeping body and soul together wasn't an easy thing at times. Soul. Heart. One and the same, he thought.

Another squeak, only this time it sounded more like a rabbit. So the owl would really have a feast if he'd caught a bunny. Tavish was glad his niece, Meagan, didn't know owls ate bunnies. She'd be all for getting her father's shotgun from the mantel and killing them all. The next noise raised every dark hair on Tavish's head. It came from a woman and the harsh whisper that followed let him know she was in danger.

He palmed his gun from the holster on the side of his hip, and eased toward the rustling leaves.

"You make a sound, even another whimper, woman and I'll kill you dead. Then I'll go back up there and reach under that wagon and take that little girl you all are so fond of. So you going to make a sound?"

Gypsy shook her head. She'd have to fight her way out of this and she didn't know if even she could win against someone the size of Goliath. She remembered the Bible stories of how the little bitty David had killed the big giant with a stone and instantly felt under her for a rock. Nothing. Not one thing.

"You filthy dirty piece of dirt," she hissed when he took his hand from her mouth. Maybe words would have to do for a stone if she didn't have a real one.

He slapped her. Openhanded across the face, splitting her lip. She tasted blood. "Shut your mouth. I didn't steal you so you could be hateful. I saw you taking a bath out there with those other two. Would've rather had that redhead but you'll do. They'll never even look for you. No one cares much for them what has Indian blood."

Her stomach lurched at the idea of this vile man looking at her and her two sisters as they bathed. Her skin crawled as if it were covered with red ants, and hot rage joined with pure old embarrassment to fill her cheeks with brilliant red color. He'd watched them. Seen them with no clothes on. "You repulsive excuse for humanity," she spat at him.

He doubled up his fist, then thought better of it. He had the advantage, after all. Big John wasn't dumb even if he'd never had any schooling. He'd told those other seven that he'd steal one of them women for them to use on the rest of the trip to Fort Bridger, and by golly he'd done it. He'd planned on snatching her out from under that wagon when she went to sleep, but she'd walked right into his arms. When he got back to their own camp, he'd show them just who was the smartest of the lot.

He'd pinned her arms with his strong legs and sat on her stomach when he tossed her on the ground like an animal he'd just killed and brought home for supper. She wasn't all Indian, now that he could see her eyes by the moon's light. No, just a half breed. That was even worse than being an Indian. Neither side would want her. What on earth was she doing on that wagon train of brides going to California, anyway? Wasn't a decent white man out there going to be willing to take her for his wife. Good Lord, he'd be doing all of them a favor by snatching her.

"I thought about having you for myself before I give you to the rest of them," he whispered, his foul breath gagging her. "But it's too close. You might scream after all, and then I'd have to snap your neck. A dead squaw wouldn't be worth much to any of us. Least I'll get my turn after they're done."

"You are a fool," she hissed, trying to wiggle free of those massive legs. If she could get an arm loose, she'd poke a finger through his eye and right into the place where his brain should have been if he'd been born with one. Or if she could free up a leg, she'd show him a good kicking.

"Yes, I think you are," Tavish said, putting the barrel of his gun against the man's temple. "A complete fool. Now I would advise you to stand up real easy like or else my finger might get nervous. When it gets nervous it quivers, and even someone as big as you are can't take a bullet in the brain without dying."

"I'll kill her," Big John said, the cold barrel against his head producing more sweat than a hard day on the road.

"Go ahead," Tavish said. "It will be the last thing you ever do."

"Why do you care, anyway?" Big John asked. "She's just a squaw."

"No, sir, she's not," Tavish said. "And if I was you, I'd not say that too loud. The last man who called her a squaw barely escaped with his throat unslit."

"I ain't scared," Big John said.

"Good. Now get up real easy. No cute stuff or I'll shoot. I don't care if you live or die, feller," Tavish pressed the gun tighter against his head.

The man started to stand and Tavish's trigger finger did tremble. The man looked like a good-sized grizzly bear. Tavish took a step back and pointed the gun where he figured his heart would be. He wouldn't trust even a bullet to go that far up and put the man on the ground before he could hurt Gypsy in a rage born of the pain of a gunshot wound to the head. No, he'd have to shoot him in the heart if he planned to drop him on the spot.

"I'm going to turn around and walk away from you," Big John said. "We wanted a woman to keep us happy on our trip to Fort Bridger. Guess I lost the game and you won, little man. You and that gun. Our paths might cross another time and I'll rip your sorry little head off with my bare hands."

"You keep walking and I'll not shoot. Turn around and I plan to send you for a close visit with the devil," Tavish told him.

"You sorry, smelly . . ." Gypsy mouthed as she found her footing and stood up. "Men like you should have never been born."

"Take her back," Big John waved over his back. "Maybe I'm lucky not to have her."

"Are you hurt?" Tavish asked, not taking his eyes from the giant.

"Just my pride," she said, drawing her arms tightly

around her, trying to ward off the evil still in the brush from that man.

"Well, that will heal. Now tell me exactly what are you doing out here disobeying Hank's orders? Huh? Can you tell me that?" Tavish kept his gun trained on the back of the man mounting a big black horse. If the fool decided to charge them, he'd have the very devil of a time trying to put him down with one shot.

"I just wanted to be quiet," she said, petulantly.

"Was it worth it?" He listened intently until the sound of horse hooves faded into the night air.

"No, it was not, Tavish O'Leary. Every time I try to find some peace and quiet, I find you instead," she said.

"Well, I guess we're even now, Gypsy Dulan. You killed a snake that threatened my life. I've killed one that did the same to you." He shoved his gun back down in the holster.

"I guess so," she said, swiping at the blood from her lip; it showing a black streak across her hand and on her night rail where she absentmindedly wiped it away.

"Gypsy!" He rushed to her side, grabbed her chin in his palm and turned her to get better light to see her with. "What did he do?"

"He slapped me when I called him names," she said, her resolve and toughness melting under the touch of his hand. A river of tears flowed from the dam behind her blue eyes and mixed with the blood running down her lip. "He said I was just an old squaw," she sobbed into her hands, unwilling to look at Tavish, who'd said the same thing the first time he saw her.

"I'm so sorry, Gypsy," Tavish held her tightly against his chest. She fit so well there, their hearts beating in unison. He patted the back of her head where her hair was parted to make two braids. "I'm so very sorry. He's just an ignorant, stupid man with no morals or care of the women in this world."

"But Tavish, no man is going to want me. When we get

there, they're all going to look at me like he did," she continued to sob.

"Gypsy, look at me," he tilted her chin up. Lord, it was nice to look at a woman shorter than he was, to feel like he was six-feet tall and bulletproof when he held her in his arms. "You are a lovely lass, and there's a man out there waiting for someone with lovely blue eyes and a sassy walk. I'm sorry I called you a squaw. Accept my apologies, please. Now let's get you back to camp before someone wakes and finds you missing."

"You're sure?" she said, the tears slowing down a little bit.

"I'm sure," he drew her back for one more hug. Just one more time to let his emotions run rampant through his heart, soul and body.

"Okay," she said. "Tavish, can we not tell what happened?"

"What are we going to tell about the cut on your lip and the condition of your night rail?"

"I busted my lip when I raised up, on the undercarriage of the wagon. I can take care of the night rail. I'll hide it and wash it tomorrow night," she said.

While she talked he leaned forward and brushed a gentle kiss across the cut. Just one to help it heal, like his mother did when he was hurt. Only somehow, it didn't feel like one of his mother's kisses. Even in the gentleness, it caused his whole world to explode in a blast of beauty.

Gypsy wasn't prepared for the touch of his lips on hers again. She was in the business of fabricating a lie when his lips touched hers. Barely. Just a whisper of a kiss. No more touching than if it had been the lightest of butterfly wings on the painful lip. Then a burst of warmth in the pits of her stomach that caused her to moan.

"We'd better go," he said hoarsely, taking her arm in his and guiding her through the brush. "It didn't mean anything, Gypsy. The kiss. It was just one of those things that happen when the fear is raging inside the body. Like we have to prove we're still alive even though we've faced the snakes or the devil, himself. It won't happen again."

"You are so right," she said. But her heart lay like a stone in her chest. Would her waiting husband's kisses affect her like that? Would he kiss her passionately and make her legs weak? Would he kiss her so softly she'd barely feel it and create a fire in her soul?

She went to sleep, finally. But her heart wasn't at peace.

## *Chapter Six*

Tavish O'Leary was in love.

It was a miserable concept, but he admitted it. He'd gone and fallen in love with Gypsy Dulan after two kisses and that was that. He'd just simply have to get himself out of love the same way he'd gotten into it. He rationalized the whole situation as he rode along that morning. He'd heard that love was blind but it was also stone deaf and dumber than a cross-eyed mule if it made him fall for the most unacceptable woman on the face of God's great green earth. Faith and the saints, he could have fallen for anyone in the world but that short, sassy woman with an opinion about everything. Besides all that, Gypsy was already spoken for even if she didn't know who her husband would be at the end of the trip. She was the same as an engaged woman and Tavish's Irish upbringing didn't allow for that. Neither did his own pride and integrity.

The Dulan women were deep in discussion when he rode up beside their wagon. Garnet and Gussie walked along beside the wagon pulled by two teams of plodding oxen. Tavish was surprised they hadn't named the creatures. Some of the women had and spoke to them like they were children. But then, on second thought, he could scarcely see Gypsy naming a big ox. Now a horse, that would be a different matter. He'd seen the way her eyes traveled over the horse he rode. Something like love or envy; maybe both. She'd mentioned that her people raised horses, so she'd know a good chunk of horse flesh when she saw it. And with all the pride a short Irishman could dig out of his soul, Tavish had to admit he was proud of his mount. It had been the first good horse he'd bought, and was the stud for a good many mares at his small but growing and very prosperous horse operation in northern Utah.

"Someday they're going to see how easy it is to cross over these mountains going through this pass, and build a railroad," Gypsy said from the wagon seat where she handled the reins with ease and confidence.

"Sure they are," Tavish chuckled. She, on the wagon seat; him, on the horse. They were on an even level. He could see the swelling on her lower lip, the cut showing very little from the outside. "And which sister hit you this morning for your sass?" he asked with a broad wink.

"None of them," she fought back the blush. "Nobody hits me and gets away with it."

"Oh?" He raised a dark eyebrow. "Then what's that cut on your lip this morning, lass? Would I dare to ask what the other person looks like? Is there a body back there waiting for the buzzards, one with his throat cut from ear to ear? Did he call you a squaw?"

"I sat up too quickly after a nightmare and bumped it on the wagon," she lied glibly, her eyes daring him to say another word in front of her sisters.

"I see. Well it must be that cut that's making you talk so big about a railroad. If it wasn't for it, you'd be knowing better," Tavish said, a gleam still in his eye.

"And who died and made you the authority on railroads?" she quipped right back. "This pass is a good fifteen miles wide. A railroad could be built through here with great ease, and it would carry the people back and forth. Why, there's enough room to make towns right here in the pass and build a station and an inn like the Patee House in

St. Joseph. Someday, I'll ride a rail car though here and when I do, I'm going to laugh at you, Tavish."

"By that time you will be so old you won't even remember the late summer when you met me. And if you could see this pass in the winter, you'd sure not be thinking of some poor fool building a hotel here. No one could get here to stay in it. Besides there's a war on the wind, Gypsy Rose Dulan. Didn't you hear of the idea down there in your rich house with your rich grandparents? To build the kind of railway you are thinking about would take a united country, not two halves fighting against themselves."

"If they'd let women have the vote, there wouldn't be a war," Gypsy smarted off at him. "We have more sense than men. All they think about is war."

At that Tavish did throw back his head and laugh. "Yes, and to be sure the day they let the women vote, we won't have a country any more. Women don't have the brains for politics. How could they ever keep their minds away from dresses and babies long enough to learn about voting?"

Gypsy shot him a drop-dead-in-your-tracks look. "And I suppose since you are a male you know exactly what it takes to run a country, keep it out of war, and build a railroad too. Can you walk on water too?"

"Of course, I know what it'll take to run a country and all those other things too. However, the railroad will have to wait, lass, because the war has to come first to free up all those slaves in your precious south so they can build the railroad," he said. "And I wouldn't know if I could walk on water. I haven't tried it yet."

"Well, try it tonight when we stop. There's a river over there. Just step right out on the top of it. Even your puffed up ego wouldn't keep you afloat, Tavish. You'd sink like a rock."

Gussie and Garnet walked along beside the wagon, listening and smiling. Looked like their baby sister had done met her match and didn't need any help from them in taming the handsome black Irish. At least, until he mentioned slaves.

"I'm from the south and so is Garnet. One of us from Tennessee, the other from Arkansas. We don't have slaves and neither did Gypsy. And that's not what this war is really about, is it?" Gussie said.

"Would you be asking or arguing?" Tavish's mouth tilted upward in a smile.

"I'm stating facts. The war is coming for sure," Gussie said. "That's all the men in Tennessee wanted to talk about. Already forming militias and getting ready for it. Slavery isn't right. To own one person, no matter what the color of their skin, isn't right. But the real reason the war is coming has little to do with that. It's a political mess for sure and it will rip at our country. Like Gypsy said, if we women had any control we wouldn't give our sons and our husbands to the war machine."

"But what if they wanted to go?" Tavish asked.

"There wouldn't be a war for them to go to," Garnet said, throwing up her hands impatiently. "We'd take care of the voting so the right people were in office. We'd find a way to end slavery without some kind of massive blood-letting. But you wouldn't understand, Tavish O'Leary. You or no other man would understand the idea that there could be a peaceful understanding."

"And why not?" Tavish asked.

"Because your brains aren't formed right in your heads," Gypsy said. "You think like a big old male mountain lion. If it gets in your way, whip it or kill it and eat it. If it's a female, it's only good to reproduce more just like you. Men are just glorified animals."

"And women?" Tavish didn't like what she'd said. Maybe if she kept talking such nonsense, falling out of love with her wouldn't be so hard after all.

"Women are a notch above men," Gypsy said. "That's why we can't vote or hold office. If we could, men would soon learn that we can think better than they can and it would blow the wind out of their egos."

"You really believe that?" he asked through clenched teeth.

"Yes, I do," she said.

"Next thing you know, you women will be wanting to do the jobs of men and hold down jobs."

"We already do," Gussie said. "Ain't a woman on this train that couldn't hold down a job, run a house and keep a garden all at the same time. They do it every day, Tavish O'Leary. Think about it. You go off to the north forty to plow your fields. We stay home. Cook your meals. Clean your house. Mend your clothing. Have your children and take care of them. Oft as not take care of the ailing women or men in the community. And if need be, we can hitch up a plow and keep up with you in the fields."

"So you think you are equal with men?" Tavish asked.

"Of course not," Gypsy said, the smile hurting her lip but figuring it was worth every single sharp pain. "We're better than men." His Irish lilt thickened as his anger mounted. She'd have to remember that in the future. Upset his perfect world and his Irish brogue got worse. It would be interesting to see if she could goad him into talking pure Gaelic.

"Well now, and that's a fine attitude to be takin' to California to your new husbands," Tavish said coldly.

"Oh, get off your high horse, Tavish," Garnet said. "We know we're better than men. Right down in the pits of our hearts, we know it, but knowing it doesn't mean we'd let them know we know. We're so good they'll never have an idea that we know we're smarter and can do more. It's the way we're made. We can know without flaunting it around. We aren't banty roosters."

"Oh, and you'd be sayin' we are?" he asked.

"Don't be twisting my words. I'm trying to explain," Garnet said. "Women are made stronger than men in the heart and in the mind. Men are made stronger in the body for the most part. It takes both to put together a union. Evidently God planned it that way, though I haven't ever figured out why."

"Well, I'll drop back and use my stronger body to protect your hearts and minds ladies," Tavish tipped his hat and pulled up the reins. When the wagon train was well ahead of him, he kneed his horse into a slow walk. Falling out of love with a Dulan woman shouldn't be so very difficult. They were all three full of themselves, thinking like that. No man alive on the face of the great green earth would ever believe all that nonsense about men's minds and hearts. Yes, and to be sure, they were as strong as a woman's. What woman would go to a war, leave her loved ones at home, and bloody well fight the enemy with guns, knives, or whatever was at hand, to protect what was hers? Not a one of them he told himself as he watched Gypsy handle the wagon and oxen team with ease. Not a one of them.

At nooning Hank rode from the front of the train back to the tail end to have his meal with Annie. Tavish joined them and listened as they discussed the snow-capped mountains on both sides of them. A cooler wind cut through the pass bringing welcome relief from the blistering hot days they were used to. Merry dreamed about hiking up the side of the mountains and eating ice cream made with thick cream, sugar and lots of clean white snow. Hank ruffled her hair and reminded her that those mountains were 15 miles away and that was just to the base of them. To climb all the way to the top where the snow was, would take more than one day.

The bean patties and biscuits, along with a pot of hot, black coffee, strong enough to melt a silver spoon, were soon eaten, and the 30-minute nooning over. Tavish wanted to rekindle the conversation, use his Irish debating wiles and convince all the girls in the last wagon on the trail that he was right and they were dead wrong. But even an Irishman knew better than to argue with a fence post, and they were as set in their thinking as a solid oak fence post. No amount of arguing would ever make them see that men were created stronger in all areas so they could protect their precious women.

Gypsy sat with her back to the wagon wheel. The day had drug on and on, seeming to never have an end. No clouds dotted the sky for her to imagine into various shapes. Only a wide pass with a gradual decline, snow-capped mountains on each side and a bit of a cooler wind wandering aimlessly through the pass. They'd passed a wooden marker declaring that two women, Eliza Hart Spalding and Narcissa Whitman, were the first white women to come that far west. From this point on, those two women had been as important as their men folks, cutting a wide swath for more women to follow. Twenty-five years ago, no white woman had ever gone that far. In 25 more years women would make even more strides in the course of history. Fifty years and she wouldn't be a bit surprised if women were standing at the polls. She'd love to be alive to see that sight, and hoped Tavish O'Leary was somewhere so she could see his face the first time she stepped right up to the polls and cast her ballot for president of the United States. Would it really be a United States by that time? Or would the south really secede, a war be fought, and there be two countries? She shook her head at that idea. There might be a war, but there wouldn't be division.

"Hello, Miss Dulan," Tavish said, tipping his hat and riding on past her.

"Mr. O'Leary," she said coldly. Tonight he was a bull-headed man; not a gentle fellow who'd made her senses reel when he kissed her like before. Maybe he'd been right after all when he said that it was just the body's way of making sure it was still alive after such a scare.

Days passed sometimes without her seeing the men who helped Hank, so why did Tavish appear every time she looked up? The tip of an iceberg called anger filled her breast. Her heart did one of those silly flip-flops when it saw him, reliving the two kisses they'd shared. It reminded her of the war she'd been thinking about. There would be one, no doubt, especially in her own soul, where Tavish O'Leary was concerned. But in the end she'd win; her heart, soul and mind would be united again, and life would go on. She would have control. When Tavish rode off to his horse ranch in some place called Chalk Creek, Utah, he would be out of sight and out of mind.

"Evenin' Gypsy," he rode past again.

"Tavish," she nodded but didn't even look up at him, riding so handsomely on that roan horse. Both more handsome than was decent. Her own big black horse had to be left in Texas. She'd raised the mare from a colt, halter broke her in her second year, and landed on her backside more than once when she was saddle training the old girl. By the time she left, she and the horse were one as she rode across the flatlands of south Texas. Beauty came close to reading Gypsy's mind; Gypsy gave her the respect and honor due a fine riding mare. Lord, she missed that horse so badly, it set her teeth on edge.

He rode on, and she yearned to walk out through the night air toward one of those mountains. Oh, she wasn't foolish enough to think she'd actually reach one of them, but the restlessness building inside her wanted to be away from the constant hum of the wagon train getting ready for bed. A few dark clouds toyed with the idea of shading the moon, but in the end the moon scared them away. Stars flickered in their stations. Did they ever get restless and want to find another place to sit? She wondered. Now that was a crazy notion, she shook her head.

"Mind if I sit a while?" Tavish asked.

"Free country. You draw the short straw and have to ride first watch?" she asked, almost glad for company to take her mind from the heavy things weighing down her mood.

"Yes, I did," he said. "Bobby says he's thinking the Indians in this area are restless. I'll ride single watch until midnight. Then they'll double team until first light. Just a precaution."

"How's he know that?" Gypsy tucked a lock of hair back into the chignon on the back of her neck.

"It's his job. He's the scout, and he knows many Indian languages. He rides out ahead and tells Hank where the best places are to go, but that's not all of his job. He keeps a close ear to the ground for any kind of danger," Tavish said, amazed that they'd said more than two sentences without a fight. He wanted to hold her hands down so she couldn't touch those errant strands of jet-black hair. The stray wisps blowing gently in the breeze added to Gypsy's mystical beauty. He could picture her in flowing scarves and dancing around a gypsy bonfire, and him tangling his hands in all that lovely black hair as he danced with her.

"I see," Gypsy said.

"So you restless tonight too?" Tavish asked.

"Sure, it's the squaw in me," she smarted off.

"You said that, I didn't," he said, bracing his back on the other half of the wagon wheel. Sitting close enough he could smell the faint aroma of roses that always went with Gypsy. He wondered if just naming a little girl child, Rose, could make her carry the rose scent with her.

"Yes, I'm restless. I handled all of this fairly well when I could sneak off for a little quiet every night. Now, I'm afraid. I keep seeing that wicked man's eyes, smelling his foul breath. I am stifled, about ready to explode with it all."

He could feel her longing to be out there with nothing but darkness and stars surrounding her. Only the sounds of nature floating on the cool night breeze to her ears. "You? Scared? I thought Dulan women could face a forest fire with only a cup of water and a solid determination to put it out."

"Oh, we could do that. Forget the water. We'd stomp it out in our bare feet. A fire is a natural force. Something we can see and deal with. It's fear that's hard to face."

"You're talking about something more than the giant

who grabbed you, Gypsy," he said, yearning to take her hand in his, to reassure her that whatever alarm kept her glued to the wagon wheel would pass with the night, and the sun's bright rays splitting through the dawn would erase it.

"I don't know who I am," she said bluntly.

"Well, now that's an easy struggle to get you out of," he laughed easily. "You are Maria Marguerite Gypsy Rose Dulan.

"That's my name. But who am I? I was that woman in Texas. I had family and a name, both honored among the people there. When I walked down the streets in town, women stopped to visit, men tipped their hats in respect. Now I'm mistaken for an Indian squaw. There is no respect. When I get to California, will it be the same?"

"Still got that on your shoulder?" he said softly. "You hold your head up, Gypsy. When you get there, you command the respect by being yourself. You are the daughter of Jake Dulan. A big man who was brave, honest and could hold his head up with dignity."

"Did you know him?" she asked, turning her head slowly to look him.

"Of course, I knew Jake. I started working the wagon trains when I was eighteen. Making money for my own place. At twenty I bought a few acres. At twenty-one, I put a cabin on it. Nothing as fancy as what you lived in, I'm sure. But it's got a nice big room that is the kitchen and living room. A fireplace in both ends. A real cook stove and a room off to the side for a bedroom. There's a loft upstairs, and lots of room to add on later when I need it. At twenty-two, I bought my first horse. Now the money from this trip will buy me the last two mares for my herd. Every one of those trips I showed up at Ash Hollow and worked the train to Echo Canyon. Every one I rode with Jake Dulan. So yes, I knew your father. He was a fine man. You don't have to be ashamed of Dulan blood."

She didn't answer him. Her eyes fixed on the far dark

horizon, illuminated by only a half moon. This Irishman, with his gift of gab, knew more about her flesh and blood father than she did. Something about that just didn't seem right. In a few minutes, he mounted his horse and rode away without saying anything more. Most likely, feeling sorry for her, that she'd never known Jake Dulan like he did.

"Gypsy, you going to sleep tonight, or sit out there and wait for some profound secret to fall out of the stars into your lap?" Gussie asked as she prepared her bedroll, out away from the wagon, toward the center of the camp.

"I'll sit here a while longer. Toss my roll under the wagon. When I get sleepy I'll curl up in it," Gypsy said without looking back.

"Okay, but remember you don't drive tomorrow. You have to walk, and there's no such thing as a nice lazy afternoon nap," Gussie reminded her. "Goodnight, little sister. There's no secrets up there, you know. The old gypsy woman was just telling you that blarney for her own reasons."

"Goodnight, Gussie," Gypsy said softly. What Paqui said, well, that had all come true in so many words. There were secrets up there that Gussie had no idea about. But she'd have to find them for herself.

"Still awake?" Tavish said after he'd made a couple more rounds.

She nodded as he dismounted again and took up the vigil with her. His back to the wagon wheel; hers right beside him. They sat in comfortable silence for several moments.

"Was he funny? Sad? Quiet, talkative? What was he like?" she asked.

"Could be all of those things," Tavish said. "Could entertain us all with stories all night long. Told about Willow's mother one night. Said he already had four daughters and had sworn off women forever, then there was this beauty that just took his breath away. Said he could see sons looking just like her. Then before he knew it they were married and didn't like each other. Told us about her sharp tongue and how he'd sneak off to the saloon and hope she'd be gone when he got home. They really, really didn't like each other."

"And did he talk about my mother?" Gypsy asked, then wished she hadn't. She'd built theirs to be a wonderful love in her imagination all those years. He was heartbroken when his poor Maria died so he had no choice but to leave his beloved daughter and ride away to find his fortune. Jake Dulan was a wonderful man in her dreams. One who would someday return and take her away with him. Only it hadn't worked that way at all. The day she received the letter from Hank, along with a stagecoach ticket and money for meals along the way, she'd almost lost the dream. When she arrived in St. Joseph, Missouri to find Jake dead and the funeral planned for the next day, the dream was buried with him. She'd never know her father. Sitting there, part of her wanted to hear what Tavish might tell her about her own mother and the part she'd played in Jake's five-wife trek though marriage. The other part wanted to keep the dream alive that she'd made up as a child.

"Yes, he did," Tavish said. "She was the pretty Mexican señorita he talked about. The one who gave him a son, proving that he could make a boy child. When he talked about her his voice grew soft and his eyes misty."

"Are you telling me the truth?" She whipped around to look at him. Her nose barely inches from his, she searched his eyes and found blatant, yet soft, honesty.

"Of course I am. He also said she was a spitfire that kept him on his toes. That he couldn't wait to come home at night and have another row with her so they could make up. He said of all his wives, Maria would have been the one he would have liked to have lived with until his old age. That, of course, was looking back and hindsight is the only one that is perfect," Tavish said. "Now I have to go ride around the camp a few more times, Gypsy Rose. You need to go get some sleep. Tomorrow is another day of journey toward the man who will make you happy."

"Tomorrow is another day of journey," she said with a curt nod. "Thank you, Tavish, for telling me about him."

"You are welcome," he said as he rode off into the night again.

"But I'm not going toward the man who will make me happy," she whispered as she crawled under the wagon and nestled down into her bedroll, pulling the blanket tightly up under her chin. "Because he isn't there. Not in California. I feel it in my bones and most of all in my heart, Tavish O'Leary."

She dreamed of a small horse operation in green fields. She rode her big black horse, Beauty, and surveyed all that was hers. A comfortable, quiet, love for the land filled her breast in the dream. The land, so very different, it was, than the flat, hot land in southern Texas. But it brought peace in her heart to be on it, and when she awoke at first dawn the next morning, she ached to go there. To know that kind of contentment for the rest of her days.

## *Chapter Seven*

The moon was a scythe without a handle, stingy with its light for Gypsy to harvest the rose petals she'd discovered earlier that evening. Thorns, serving as guards against thieves wishing to rob the bush of its glory, stuck Gypsy's fingers and brought forth a string of Spanish she was glad her grandmother couldn't hear. She was determined to win the thorn war and have every one of those red petals to carry along to her new home. She eased away a few more petals, whispering to the rose bush in Spanish that it would soon be throwing them on the ground anyway, so why not share with her.

When the pillowcase was half full of petals and the bush picked clean, she chose the hips with the most orange in them and pocketed the little round balls. She'd find a dry place to keep them until frost came, then she would harvest the seeds from within. They'd stay inside a jar full of good, dark soil on the back porch until spring time when the warmth of the sun would make them sprout. Like all new things—babies and love included—they'd be fragile and she'd have to work hard at keeping them watered until they were six-inches tall. Then she could plant them out along the yard fence. It would be at least three years before she saw blooms. Maybe by then she'd be adapted to the new surroundings. Maybe by then she wouldn't remember the kisses that she shared with Tavish O'Leary. Maybe by then she wouldn't be in love with him anymore.

Love with him!

A thorn reached out and bit her on the thumb. Instinctively, she stuck it in her mouth. Love with Tavish? Now that was one crazy thought. She wasn't in the same place Willow had been when she fell for Rafe. Hank and Rafe were best friends so there hadn't been a problem with him marrying one of the brides who was under contract to marry another man. Unless there were a hundred other women when they reached Bryte, Gypsy had given her word that she'd stand right up there before the preacher man and marry the man who'd paid her passage from St. Joseph, Missouri to California. It didn't matter that she loved Tavish. She'd just have to unlove him . . . if that was possible. At the least, she'd have to bury that love deeply in her heart and never speak of it again.

Paqui said that love quickened all the senses. Well, it didn't do a blasted thing for common sense. If she'd had a lick of common sense she wouldn't have let herself fall in love with the most unacceptable man who ever sucked air into his lungs. Tavish O'Leary was the exact opposite of the man of her dreams. With his shiny dark hair, sparkling black eyes and all that blarney he put out, why, he could most likely talk a nun into kissing him. But Gypsy had been running from men with those qualities for years, so what had happened? Her silly heart had done just what Gussie warned her of a few nights before. It hadn't used her eyes to see, or her mind to understand. It had simply fallen in love without any discussion.

She sighed deeply as she made a small fire beneath the limbs of an oversized tree. Green leaves would capture the smoke and hold it like Tavish held her when he kissed her the first time.

"Have to stop it," she murmured. "Can't keep letting

everything remind me of him. I'll have to make a real effort not to let this go any further."

She filled a bucket from the river and set it above the flames. While she waited for the water to reach a boil, she let a Spanish love song play from start to finish through her mind. When the last strains of the imaginary guitar strummed the final chord, she swayed with the warm night air and let it begin again, only this time she sang softly with the music playing only in her heart and head. It was a sad song of a señorita who loved her man so much that when he died in the war, she laid down on his grave and let the angels have her soul.

That song brought another to mind, and she sang it as she dipped her hand into the pillowcase, fingering the velvety-soft rose petals for a while before she dropped them into the boiling water. Rose water for both her sisters as well as Annie. Perhaps to dab on their wrists and behind their ears on the day of their marriage.

She bent low over the sweet smell of the roses giving up their oil and fragrance to the boiling water and breathed deeply. Paqui said the aroma of roses heightened her power to see the future. The rose water was for her sisters; the power, Gypsy craved for her own self. To end the indecision and confusion. To give her just one little vision of what man she would have to spend the rest of her life with.

She opened her eyes but there was no sight. Nothing. She remembered seeing her old gypsy friend sway in the wind and sing a hauntingly beautiful song at a wedding once. Gypsy didn't know the words, but by deep concentration she could hear the tune well enough to hum it. She was much too restless to simply sway so she hummed the tune and danced around the glowing fire.

That's what Tavish saw when he looked up. He was struck senseless by the sheer grace and energy before him. The fragile yet exotic movements mesmerized him. He dropped to his knees and then even further, resting his elbows in the grass. Well hidden in the sage brush, he dropped his chin into his hands and watched, holding his breath so long his lungs ached. She was the wind as she twirled, keeping time to a song sounding both sad and ethereal. If angels fell from the white puffy clouds and played their harps, that's what they would look and sound like, he decided. The stars were at her beck and call, dropping down from heaven to glisten in the moon's light on her black hair, escaping its hair pins and flowing around her shoulders, no less than a perfect halo. Her arms were liquid grace as they told the tale in movements of the melody she hummed. Tavish was afraid to blink for fear she would disappear. His heart twisted up into a knot with love. Love that he could never have. Love that wasn't his to ask for, to court. The loneliest place in the world, Tavish learned while he watched his Mexican angel, was the human heart in love with one it could not have.

The dance stopped. The glorious angelic humming, also. Using the tail of her blue skirt tail, she picked up the bucket by the bail and set it off the fire to cool. When she could, she'd strain the water into four quart jars she'd brought along. The beautiful petals had given their all, and were nothing but browned leaves now with no lovely smell; no velvet in their touch. But someday, when Gussie and Garnet used the water on themselves it would be reincarnated. The smell would bring them and their husbands great joy. It would make them feel like velvet, even if they were wearing calico.

She sniffed the night air, taking in a lung full of the lovely rose scent. Too bad, it hadn't worked for her the way it did Paqui. Evidently she didn't have the sight and most likely that was for the best. If she could have seen the man she would have to promise to love, honor and obey—that last word stuck in her throat like a two-day old biscuit—and he wasn't to her liking, it would have made the journey even worse.

She started to kick dirt over the tiny fire she'd built, but the embers captured her attention. The song came back to her; she began to hum again. She raised her arms and let the melody sweep her back into the time when she went to a wedding for Paqui's granddaughter. The bride and groom had danced to this tune and when it was done, with his hand over hers, they'd opened the gilded cage where a white dove was held captive. With hands still held, they'd watched the dove fly out of captivity and toward the quarter moon. Paqui said later the dove would take their love all the way to the moon and it would be cherished there in the cradle forever.

She twirled around the fire, like the bride had done, teasing her husband with a long scarf made of pure blue liquid. Only Gypsy's scarf was totally in her imagination. At least she thought it was. Tavish could see the scarf in the semi-light as clearly as if she were actually holding it. Whatever she was brewing in that rose-scented pot, and for whatever reason, he certainly wasn't going to disturb her. Not tonight. He rose to his knees and then to his feet, planning to slip back to the camp and leave her alone.

At least until he stood up and her eyes met his across the few feet separating them. His feet were glued to the spot where he stood and although common sense told him to turn tail and run as fast as he could back to the camp, his heart wouldn't let him budge. She looked up and smiled, beckoning him to join her. He walked slowly forward until he was standing in front of her. She twirled twice, wrapped her arms around his neck, and the two of them danced the wedding dance together around the dying embers of the fire. When the last of the music faded from her mind, she looked up to see Tavish O'Leary's eyes boring into hers with such fierce intensity, it rooted her to the ground where she stood.

She must be dreaming. Surely she had not really seen him standing out there in the deep shadows and beckoned to him to join her in the most private and ritual of all gypsy dances. He didn't look like a vision though. He looked and felt real, muscles bulging across his back where her hand rested. The callused hand holding hers loosely, causing a sizzle in the air around them, didn't feel like an illusion. His heart, beating in perfect unison with her own—a bit too fast and trying to tell them something important—certainly didn't come from a man made of smoke and wishes. His lips coming toward her were full and begging to blend with hers.

The kiss was as sweet as the soft one he'd placed on her mouth when he'd rescued her from the evil man; as wild and passionate as the one he'd put there when she'd killed the snake. Warmth seethed through every sense as well as her body, and she ached for the kiss to never end.

"I'm sorry," he said, breaking away, turning his back on her.

"For what? Seems like I was so taken up in the memories of a dance that I invited you into it."

"I cannot care for you, Gypsy. I cannot. It's not just my job. It's my dignity. You are promised to another man. I will not dishonor that. I can not and live with myself. I'm going back to the camp now. Please don't stay out here much longer being a Mexican angel. It's late." He disappeared into the darkness, his shoulders sagging with the weight of a four-letter word called love.

She kicked dirt over the fire with such vengeance she could have put out a full fledged forest fire. So he couldn't care for her? What was he doing out there anyway, spying on her while she tried desperately to have a vision? Evidently, roses didn't enhance the psychic ability. If it did, she sure wouldn't look up and see Tavish O'Leary out there in the shadows, watching her dance. No sir, she wouldn't have seen him at all.

Whatever possessed her to hold her arms out to him, asking him to take the groom's part, had passed quickly after that kiss, which sent sparks from the embers of the fire to dance around them in a shower of falling fire and light. One moment she was a feather, lifted ever so gently on the soft summer breeze toward heaven. The next she was thrown to earth like a stone dropped from 50 feet up in a tall tree. The lightness of the heart afloat disappeared and all that remained was a dirty old rock inside Gypsy's heart. She'd made a fool of herself.

"Well, well, did the stargazer make it back in time for a few hours of sleep?" Gussie mumbled when Gypsy crawled into her bedroll.

"I wasn't stargazing," Gypsy said. "I was making rose water so you will smell and feel like a princess on the day of your marriage. I found the roses when I went to the river for a bath, and decided I would make the rose water. I'm sorry I woke you."

"What a nice thing to do. Thank you, Gypsy. Now tell me what's wrong, little sister?" Gussie whispered. "Something went on out there, didn't it? Are you all right?"

"I'm fine, Gussie," Gypsy said. "Goodnight."

Gussie mumbled again and Gypsy was left to try to make sense of the topsy-turvy world around her. One thing was for sure, unrequited love sure made a miserable and unmerciful bed partner.

"So did you find Gypsy Dulan out there?" Bobby asked softly when Tavish plopped down, fully clothed on his own bedroll.

"Aye, I did," he said. "You about to be on watch?"

"I am. And what did she say this time with that sharp tongue to cut you into ribbons of flesh?"

"Nothing."

"And you'd expect me to believe that? I've been with this train since the beginning, Tavish. I know that girl better than you do. She wouldn't have let you get away without at least a few mean words," Bobby grinned, his white teeth shining in the darkness.

"You ever been in love Bobby?"

Bobby chuckled. "Once I got that itch in my heart so deep I couldn't scratch it. Seemed like the world was spinning around every time I got near that lovely lady with the milky white skin and blue eyes. She didn't know Bobby Whiteleaf was anything more than an Indian guide for the wagon train she was on, though. I figured out right quick that a swallow of tobacco juice could produce the same effects without the heartache. Never fell in love again. What do you intend to do about this?"

"Start chewing tobacco, I guess," Tavish said. "Faith and saints, man. There's nothing I can do about it. She's been bought by another man. She's the same as engaged. I can not do one thing about it."

"Rafe did. Married Willow and Hank even did the ceremony for them. Hank didn't make him pay up the money for Willow, either," Bobby said as he pulled on his boots.

"Rafe is Hank's neighbor in Nebraska. I am his hired hand, and besides I couldn't do that. She couldn't love me anyway, Bobby. She comes from rich people. Even old Jake told us that if you'll remember. Said as how her parents thought he was a gold digger after their horse operation. She's been spoken for by some man out west who has enough gold to pay her way there. Who'll probably have some kind of mansion built for her with maids and real crystal lights hanging from the ceiling. All I've got is a two-room cabin with a loft and enough work to last a lifetime. If she was willing, which she isn't, it would take my whole paycheck to give Hank the money back for her. And that would mean another year working the wagon trains to buy my breeding stock."

"Sounds like you got a problem. What're you going to do?"

"I'm going to sleep right now," Tavish said. "And forget all about Gypsy Rose Dulan. I'm going to stay away from her the rest of this trip, then I'm going to Chalk Creek and work hard to clear her from my mind."

"If you can do that then you might want to travel around and give lessons to men folks who've fallen for the wrong woman, Tavish," Bobby laughed. The white man's world was so much more complicated than his Indian world.

When he finished this trip, he'd winter with his people in the north, trapping, hunting, maybe even taking a wife of his own this year. But he wouldn't lay awake at night and fret about it. Yes, his world was more simple and for that he was thankful.

Tavish shut his eyes and inhaled deeply. He could still smell the hot rose petals and see Gypsy as she danced first alone and then with him. Somewhere he'd seen that dance before. Like a lightning bolt, he sat straight up, his eyes wide open. It had been when the gypsies came that summer when he was 14. A couple married and his whole family attended the wedding. The bride and groom did a dance like that, and then they opened a lovely cage and let a dove fly free.

If he closed his eyes, he could see the dance again, only this time it was Gypsy who was the bride. All the movements were there. He could even see the dove as it flew up toward the dark skies to the moon, which was to cradle and keep the love of the couple forever. Gypsy had invited him into a wedding dance and he'd danced it with her, not knowing at that time how he even knew what to do next.

Not that it mattered. She'd been caught up in the moment. Humming that song. The scent of roses permeating the night air. The seduction of the small blaze and the glowing embers. All of it had caused her to reach out to the first man she saw and to let him be her groom for a few moments. A short Irish groom that no woman like Gypsy could love in his work jeans and chambray shirt; a beautiful Mexican bride in her faded blue, swirling skirt and imaginary scarf of blue silk.

He threw himself backwards with a thud. There would be no more moments like that. "Faith and saints above," he muttered under his breath. "I've just done the wedding dance with Gypsy Dulan, and there's nothing me heart would like better than to finish a lifetime with her. But it will just have to hold tight the memory of the moment, because that's all it will ever have."

He went to sleep thinking of ways to avoid her. Things he could and would do to assure he was never in a position like that again. It wouldn't be so very difficult after all. He wouldn't go outside the camp at night. He would spend more time riding far enough behind the wagon train he couldn't see or talk to her. There was only a few more weeks to Echo Canyon and he was a wily Irishman. By the time he got home to Chalk Creek, she would just be a pleasant and fading memory.

He could run from her every day for the rest of his life.

But the night belonged to his dreams and they refused to obey him.

## *Chapter Eight*

Gypsy fought down the impulse to escape to a world of peace and quietness for the next few nights. She'd made up her mind if Tavish could avoid her, then she could certainly oblige him by doing the same. It was for the best anyway. She was contracted to another man. He was filled with Irish pride and dignity.

Both were miserable.

While Annie and Merry prepared a stew, the three Dulan sisters took the laundry for their wagon to the river. The previous day Hank had bought two beeves from a wagon train on its way to Fort Bridger to sell supplies. They'd traveled along together for a couple of hours then the four freight wagons pulled out ahead of them and disappeared before nightfall. He'd also paid an exorbitant price for a few bushels of potatoes and carrots for the ladies. Gypsy was filling her pail with wild garlic when she heard the rustling of men's boots close by. She'd filled her bucket anyway with some to dry for later seasoning in the monotonous pots of beans, and some for that night's stew. Gussie and Garnet had already gone back to the camp—Gussie carrying two buckets of water to refill the barrel on the side of their wagon; Garnet the bushel basket of wet clothes to dry on the line they'd stretch between their wagon and an oak tree.

Gypsy kept a sharp eye out for Tavish, hoping that she wouldn't get caught alone in his presence again. Goodness only knew every time she did they fought or kissed and either one sent her senses reeling. She was figuring out a way to get back to the camp without passing the men folks, one of whom might well be Tavish, when she overheard Hank and Bobby talking.

"So what do you think would be our best plan?" Hank said.

"That's your call," Bobby said. "But I think we should sleep inside the women's circle. Tell them what's about to happen and get them ready. It'll make for a fretful night, all right, but if they're prepared and it's not a surprise they'll take it better. They're tough from more than half the journey, Hank. They'll do fine. Give each wagon two rifles and tell the one who's the best shot to do the shooting. The others can keep reloading. Tell them not to be squeamish about pulling the trigger. It's their life if they don't."

Gypsy's heart jumped up into her throat and tried to choke her plumb to death. She wished she'd been content with what garlic she'd already gathered and gone on back to camp with her two sisters. Indians on the warpath! And the women were expected to take up arms and shoot them dead. She was a crack shot with a rifle when the enemy was a syrup bucket on a fence post, but she didn't know if she could actually kill a human being; even if he was a painted-up Indian who had full intentions of killing her. She'd have no choice though, because if she didn't that same human could very well kill Merry or one of the other women. She shivered at the very idea of pulling the trigger and killing a man. One who might have children and a wife waiting for him at his camp.

"Sounds like sound advice. We'll call the meeting. We'll pull two-hour guard duty just in case, but they won't hit until just at daybreak, will they?" Hank's voice sounded tired.

"No, they won't. They're camped about five miles back. At least a hundred of them. They'll be smoking their pipes tonight and hunting some kind of vision of great victory. They think we don't even know they're there, and they'll depend on a surprise to bring on that victory," Bobby said.

"You're sure you understood them right?"

"It's one of the languages I understand. They're a renegade bunch and they're out for blood and supplies. This train is a sitting duck for them, with only a handful of men and lots of women. They'll see it as an easy victory."

Gypsy's heart stopped and quivered before it knotted up in a hurting ball of fear. Real danger against her and her sisters, as well as little Merry. She could shoot the eyes out of a coyote without messing up the hide so she'd insist on being the one to hold the gun and she'd just have to brace up and pull the trigger even if it was a human head and not a shiny bucket on the top of a fence post. She'd have to protect her sisters and their friends. She'd keep her silence until Hank had his conference with the whole train, but as nervous as her stomach was, she'd never be able to eat the fine stew Annie was brewing for supper.

Hank didn't wait until after supper. He and the other men strolled into the circle, called everyone close for the news, and then delivered it, just like he and Bobby had discussed. Gypsy watched several women's color drain from their faces, leaving them a pasty white with fear. Connie laid the back of her hand on her forehead and began to moan.

"Stop it," Annie hissed. "Merry is going to have enough trouble with this without you acting like a ninny."

"Merry, nothing!" Connie wilted, dropping to her knees. "Tavish, you'll simply have to stay beside my wagon. None of us in our wagon can shoot. You'll have to take care of us."

"I can shoot," Bertie stepped forward. "I'm not afraid of a gun. You just keep it loaded."

Connie shot her a look meant to shut her up, but Bertie went on to say that she'd been shooting squirrels for years. Her brothers taught her how before they all grew up and left home, and that if she could hit a little bitty squirrel hiding on a tree limb, she reckoned she could hit a man coming at her with intentions of killing her. Tavish just smiled, but Gypsy noticed that it was a tight grin, one full of concern and worry, before he walked away to break up the camp they'd made away from the ladies. Would he be alive tomorrow at this time? Would she? And what would he think of a woman who'd just sent many men to eternity?

The women were told to put their rolls inside the circle. Men would sleep under every other wagon. Before daybreak Hank would wake them all and they'd get prepared for the first onslaught. Indians, he told them, didn't send down the whole force in one fell swoop. The first bunch would hit fast and hard, do as much damage as they could, then be riding back even as the second wave rode down and hit them again. They'd do that off and on all day until they were either diminished so much they'd crawl off and lick their wounds, or until they'd taken out every living soul on the train.

Tavish flipped out his bedding under the Dulan wagon and laced his fingers behind his head. He'd pulled the first watch, and he'd best get sleep when he could. Tomorrow was going to be a devil of a day. He'd seen Indian attacks before. A couple they'd been prepared for and the results hadn't been as bad as they could have been. Only a few people to bury when it was over. Would he have to watch Gypsy's body put down in a six-foot hole? Would he have to carve her name on a cross to mark it? She'd stepped right up and said she'd do the shooting, but Garnet thought otherwise. Garnet said she'd taken down a grizzly bear in the Arkansas mountains and didn't even leave a hole in the hide. Made a perfect rug for in front of her aunt's fireplace when Garnet got the hide tanned. Gypsy didn't like it, but she said she'd load for Garnet and relieve her when the going got tough.

He shut his eyes after a while and a restless sleep finally claimed him.

Gypsy's eyes were shut; her mind running free. What could she do? Anything at all? Hank had said they'd ride in fast and furious with lots of noise, hoping to surprise and startle all the women. Then the next wave would ride in. Ride in. Ride in. Ride in. That's where the answer lay. If they had no horses to ride in on, the first wave couldn't begin the war. They sure wouldn't appear out from under the sage brush and come running in their little moccasins toward women and men with guns trained on them.

So how did one make sure they didn't have horses? A nervous grin twitched at the corners of her mouth. She could do it. She knew she could even if it was foolhardy. That's what Garnet and Gussie would tell her. And she'd have to agree with them. Common sense told her to go to sleep and get ready for a fierce battle arriving with the first rays of sun tomorrow. But Gypsy never had been real fond of common sense. It could just be quiet because she'd made up her mind she was going to take matters in her own hands. Common sense could go sit on a barbed wire fence in Hades. Not one time had it ever accomplished the impossible, she was quite sure. And tonight Gypsy was going to have to achieve more than the impossible. She was going to have to produce a pure miracle.

Gussie sighed in her sleep. Garnet slept with her hands under her beautiful face. Annie had drawn Merry into a fierce embrace. Gypsy waited until the guard had made one round and was on the other side of the circle before she rolled out of the bedding and slipped into the back of the wagon. In the dark she rifled through her trunk and found her leather riding skirt, a flannel shirt and her old soft work boots. She braided her hair into two long ropes and let them hang over her shoulders. She worked as quietly as possible, knowing that only the thin boards of the wagon bottom separated her from Tavish. Lord, if he caught her sneaking out, there'd be the pure old devil to pay. He'd wake the whole camp with his Irish temper. She held her breath, flipping back the wagon sheet and bending low to see if he was still sleeping.

Even in his sleep he was a handsome man. Black hair falling down over his dark eyebrows. A strong jaw and angular face, with the nicest mouth she'd ever seen. One that could kiss her one minute and curse her the next. Keeping her eyes on his face, she carefully let herself out of the wagon, blessing him for sleeping like the dead and cursing him with the same breath for not waking up. Had she been an Indian, he could be dead already, along with half the sleeping women in the camp.

She heard the guard pass again, waited until he was several hundred feet away and made her way to the horses. If worse came to worse, and she got caught, she'd pretend to be a half-breed squaw. That shouldn't be so difficult. Seemed like most people these days mistook her for one anyway. The horses had been staked near the camp so they could be brought in quickly when Hank awoke the women. By closing her eyes, Gypsy could envision the coming melee inside the circular camp when the first wave of Indians came whooping down upon them. More than a hundred oxen and several horses wandering around in a tight little circle, along with all those women. How many of them would drop dead from Indian's arrows and bullets? She shuddered at the thought and kept her eyes wide open as she chose the biggest horse there, a black that Hank usually tied along with half a dozen others to the supply wagon. It rolled its eyes when she approached and reared back against the rope tether. She whispered words of comfort, reaching out her hand with a sugar cube in her palm. While the horse nibbled, she drew closer and closer until she was running her small hands down its nose and crooning Spanish in its ear. When she was content that she'd gained his confidence, she pulled up the stake and threw the rope over his back.

She grabbed a handful of black, silky mane and hoped she hadn't read the horse wrong. If he reared up and began to buck, she'd be undone. Tavish would throw a hissy fit but it wouldn't come close to the one Hank would pitch.

The horse stood perfectly still while she jumped to mount his bare back and picked up the tether rope. She kneed him gently in the ribs and turned him quickly, barely making it out of sight before the guard rode past that way again. She leaned forward until she was lying on his back, her mouth whispering Spanish promises in his ear as she rode out into the darkness, back on the trail she'd just put behind her that very day. Bobby said the Indians were camped five miles back. She'd be there in a little over an hour. Just after midnight. If everything went well, she'd be back in her bedroll long before daybreak.

She saw the thin trailing spiral of smoke reaching toward the stars in the absence of any kind of moon and dismounted her black steed. She led him in that direction, trying to keep the scarce stands of trees behind her so if their own sentry looked out she wouldn't be silhouetted in what little light the stars gave off. Thank goodness there wasn't a moon to give off its luminary light or she'd be in really big trouble. She tied the horse to a low branch of an oak tree, whispered into his ear, and dropped down on her hands and knees to crawl to the top of a small rise.

They had set up camp in a small grove of trees. The central fire blazed brightly, and lying on her stomach, peeping over the top of the brush-covered upgrade, she could easily count a hundred of them. Some were sleeping on the ground. Some were passing around a pipe as they stared into the fire and uttered words in some tongue she didn't understand. Guards seemed to be everywhere. Two kept close watch over the horses which were kept in a makeshift corral of rope stretched between two trees; another seemed to be wandering around the entire camp keeping check on everything. An Indian with paint all over his face sat with his back against one tree. What looked like his twin brother, was against the other. All she had to do was cut the ends of the rope between the trees but it just flat looked impossible to do the job alone. If they caught her before the horses where stolen, she'd be dead and the raid would still take place.

She'd simply have to figure out something else. She fingered her knife, tucked safely in the leather pouch hiding in her skirt. Mercy, but she hadn't realized how much she missed riding until she and the black beast tied to a tree not 50 feet away made their way across the sage brush. She crawfished back into the weeds; close enough to keep the whole camp in view; far enough away to catch her breath and rethink the situation.

One of the pony guards raised his head and inhaled deeply. Roses. There wasn't a rose bush out here in the brush, but a faint whiff wafted through the breeze toward him. He stood up, and waited patiently. Another sniff or two and it was still there. He took a step away from the tree and carefully looked out across the land. Nothing. Not a rose bush or anything. The only scent he could take in now was the sweet smell of the vision weed. Black Wolf said he saw great victory tomorrow. There would be supplies and cattle to take back to his people, and lots of dead women to show the white man that the Indians were not tolerating white men in his land, killing his buffalo, bringing their new ideas to wipe out Indian ways.

The Indian drew closer to the fire, taking in great whiffs of the vision weed smoke. He loved the sweetness of it and next year when he came into his manhood, he'd be given the pipe to smoke when they went to war with the white man. He and his cousin who stood guard with him would see visions of their own. He was in a hurry for the year to pass so he could ride in on the first wave of the battles. He'd love to see the white man's eyes as they came out of their sleep and saw the painted warriors coming at them. Maybe there would even be a fog tomorrow, as thick as the smoke over the camp. That would even be better. For the white man to awake and see the devilish Indians bearing down on them straight out of a smoky gray fog.

The Indian's thin mouth arched upward in a grin. His cousin joined him at the edge of the camp fire, the two of them whispering about spring rites when they'd be man enough to actually suck the smoke into their own lungs instead of relying on the second hand sweetness that hung over the camp like a misty cloud.

Gypsy saw the guards leave their posts and hoped they'd stay at the camp a while longer. She began a very slow crawl around the far reaches of their gathering, inching along a foot at a time on her belly. She just needed to get to the ponies. Cut the ropes and make a ruckus. They'd run away and she'd be right behind them. Running as fast as she could to the black horse. With no horses, the Indians would be stuck right where they were, and the wagon train could go right on down the trail. They'd never know she was out of the camp. She'd slip right back into her bedroll, and when the Indians didn't come whooping and hollering at dawn, they'd figure they'd changed their mind. She'd never tell, but her sisters, Gussie and Garnet, as well as Annie and Merry would be safe. Too bad she couldn't have kidnapped Connie and brought her along. She could have left her in trade for the ponies. The Indians would have loved that blond hair and blue eyes.

Tavish awoke with a start. Was it already morning? He let his eyes adjust to his surroundings. He was under the Dulan wagon and there was someone inside it. He listened for a while and then whoever it was, eased out the back. Apparently one of the women needed something desperately to go digging around for it so late at night. He rolled over, pulled the covers over his ears and went back to sleep.

A few minutes later, he awoke again, sweat pouring from his pores. Something wasn't right. Not that he was *fey,* had the sight, because he wasn't. But something out there was going on that wasn't quite right. He lay very still. The

Indians must be sending in a guard to check out the competition. If that guard saw one camp instead of two, he'd know they were on alert. He heard the soft whinny of a horse near the line where he'd personally staked out the livestock. Instantly, he'd pulled his boots on and was sneaking out into the darkness.

The rider was just out of sight, riding bareback on a black horse. He strained his eyes against the dim night light but all he could see was someone lying out across the horse's back, two long braids whipping around and a flash of leather around the Indian's legs. It was too late to do anything about the guard now. He'd seen what he'd seen and nothing could come of following him. Tavish went back to his bed.

He'd barely shut his eyes when that prickly sensation crawled up his neck. The same one that disturbed him when Gypsy was close by. His eyelids snapped open. Lord, that girl had better not be out there in the darkness beside the river tonight. If she was, he just might turn her over his knee and give her the spanking she deserved. He rolled out of his bed again, angry all the way to his bare feet at her. Hadn't she learned a blessed thing from her escapade into the night when the mule skinner grabbed her? In all the years of his working with the wagon trains, he'd never had so much trouble with a woman. He mumbled under his breath as he stepped out over the wagon tongue and started toward the river.

"What you doin' Tavish?" the guard whispered from out of the night as he rode past.

"Nothing, just following nature's call. It's a pain sleeping in surrounded by women," Tavish said, thinking fast. Much as it went against his grain, he wouldn't get her in trouble if he didn't have to. Besides he fully well could take care of Gypsy Dulan by himself. Even looked forward to it, if the truth be known.

"Ain't it though?" the guard chuckled. "More'n a hundred and we can't court none of them."

"Aye, 'tis the truth," Tavish said with a sigh.

The guard rode on and the sting on Tavish's neck deepened. He went back inside the camp and tiptoed over to the Dulans' bedside. Gussie was curled up in a ball, her golden hair braided, ready for battle. Garnet slept with her hands behind her neck, fully dressed, ready for battle. Merry was curled up in Annie's arms tightly, ready for battle. Gypsy was . . .

He looked again. Her bed was empty. The sight of a black horse with a rider leaning up across his back came back to his mind. Two long black braids flowing in the wind as she rode away. Good grief, that wasn't an Indian. It was Gypsy! What did she think she was going to do. Fight a hundred Indians with one little *bodkin*?

He mumbled Gaelic words so hot they'd fry Saint Lucifer's ears, and without an hour in confession would keep him in purgatory for eternity plus three days. There was nothing to do but go after her and hope to the very saints that they got back before either of them were missed. Hank would fire him on the spot for taking things in his own hands. He grabbed his saddle from under the wagon where he'd been sleeping and without making a sound, got his horse ready to go after Gypsy Rose Dulan. If they got out of this one with their bodies and souls still stuck together, then Hank had better clean off a space right in the middle of the camp, because Tavish was going to have a pure-breed Irish tantrum and Gypsy Rose was going to stand there and listen to what he had to say. If Hank did fire him, then so be it. He'd just have to work another year to buy the rest of the stock he needed to get his horse ranch underway. Rotten woman anyway. Indians on the warpath wouldn't think twice about killing her, and that little *bodkin* she carried wouldn't protect her for long.

He saw the ever-so-faint trail of smoke stretching out to the sky and dismounted, leading his horse as quietly as possible toward their campsite. A soft whinny to his left made the hair on his arms tingle. Two more steps and he found Gypsy's horse, tied very loosely to a tree limb. He tied his own mount to the same limb, whispered words of comfort into the horse's ear and began to make his way toward the camp. They'd chosen well. A grove of trees to keep the smoke at a minimum. Many sleeping. A few still passing the pipe and the sickening sweet smell of vision weed. He'd never liked it. Not even when his little Indian friend had found some in the pasture and dried it for them to smoke that year when he was 12. The friend said he saw a vision. All Tavish got was a dizzy head and a sick stomach.

Where was she? He lay on his stomach and breathed in and out as quietly as possible. Two guards left their posts beside the corral and went to stand just outside the fire, talking quietly and gesturing with their hands.

But faith and saints above, where was Gypsy?

## *Chapter Nine*

Gypsy inched along to the edge of the trees where the horses were kept and checked to see how many lines she'd have to cut before she could stampede the ponies. It ran back into the darkness to another tree and then to another one past that. She'd hoped to find a natural corral with only ropes in the front, but her luck wasn't that good. Not that night. Four ropes strung out with a good bit of distance between them, making a corral in a small clearing, and the horses' ears were already perking up with the smell of a stranger on the perimeter of their pen. In a few minutes they'd start to mill around and neigh. *When all else fails,* she thought, *regroup and rethink. But I don't have time to do either.*

As if their thoughts ran in the same vein, Tavish caught sight of her as she blended back into the tree line, studying all those horses. Surely she wasn't fool enough to think she could steal all their livestock. Faith and saints above, he bit his tongue to keep from muttering, that's exactly what she had in mind!

She'd begun to cut through the rope at the first tree when an arm clamped around her neck, the hand squeezing even the faintest scream from her mouth. The dagger was on its way to slash the hand to ribbons when Tavish whispered quickly in her ear. "Don't you make a sound, Gypsy Rose Dulan. I'm letting go now. Remind me when we get back to camp that we have a battle to fight for this fool stunt."

She swallowed the fear in her throat and fought back the sizzling warmth in her breast at the touch of his hand lying warm on her shoulder. She motioned to the other three trees. She'd get the first two if he could snip the last two. Then they would sneak back to their horses waiting just outside the camp, come riding in and stampede the Indian's mounts. The element of surprise was the only thing they had going for them. That and a hope that the ponies didn't give them away to those guards who were only yards away.

Tavish changed the plan. With motions he told Gypsy that he'd mount a pony and she was to jump on the first one she could get to once she had her part of the ropes cut. They'd start from that point, taking no chance that those Indian guards back there might make it back to their guns in time to start firing before they had a good stampede going. Gypsy nodded, but she wasn't leaving that big black beast for the Indians, either. Gypsy sincerely hoped that Tavish was as well versed in trick horsemanship as she was, because both of them would only have one chance to do what she had in mind. It was dangerous, yes. But if it worked, they'd have their own horses and wouldn't be leaving them for at least two Indians to use to gather up their own mounts with.

He nodded when she threw a leg over a paint horse that didn't seem to mind her weight. Tavish knew in his heart that he and Gypsy were both dead. He'd be laid out in the middle of Wyoming without a scrap of hair on his head. He'd die without a priest and his soul would probably linger in purgatory forever. And what was worse, it would be stalled out in that place with Gypsy Rose Dulan, because she was already graveyard dead just like he was, and wasn't even smart enough to know it even if she did spout off all that balderdash about women being so intelligent. He stooped low, used the horses for cover and cut through the ropes like Gypsy told him. If it worked they'd create a melee by stampeding a hundred animals. He and Gypsy had best stay on their mounts because if the Indians didn't shoot them with bullets or flying arrows, the horses would pound them into the earth in their quest for freedom. He'd barely slung his body up on the bare back of a buckskin-colored horse when he heard a scream that raised every hair on his head and caused his heart to skip at least three beats. The Indians had discovered Gypsy and she was already dead. An emptiness filled his chest for just a split second, until he realized the scream had come from Gypsy and she was riding hard not a dozen feet behind him, bringing on a herd of ponies so fast that he had to kick his mount sharply to keep out of her way.

He looked back in time to see an army of Indians coming out of sleep, two guards running after them, with rifles raised, and Gypsy riding bareback looking for everything like a real Indian squaw on that brown-and-white-spotted horse, her braids flying out behind her as she laid low on his back. She let out one war whoop after another, creating as much confusion as possible.

Bullets began to whiz around them in the few minutes it took to steer that pack of horses toward the two tied loosely to the branches of the tree. Tavish longingly looked ahead at his big roan and wondered if he'd ever ride on it again. If the Indians would be good to him when they claimed him for their own. Gypsy shot out ahead of him and in one easy fluid motion she jumped from the pony to the black horse, laying out over it's neck and holding on to the black silky mane. She'd done it! By golly, she'd made the jump and connected just as solidly as she'd done with all her cousins when they played horse trickery in Texas. She kicked the horse into action and kept riding, herding the horses toward the mountains in the distance. She could hear bullets whizzing past her and one horse fell, but the others either jumped over its dead body or ran around it, so eager were they to race in unbridled freedom.

Tavish saw what she'd done and in that split second before common sense could talk him out of it, he decided that if Gypsy could do it, he could, also. If he connected, he wouldn't lose his favorite horse. If he missed and landed in the dirt, he'd be trampled to death. He didn't think about it but jumped and landed firmly in the saddle, his rear end hitting with enough force to jar his tail bone, sending pain up his back all the way to the top of his head. He acknowledged the ache with a loud grunt and then he and the horse were off, right on Gypsy's tail, the thundering hooves of a stampede of horses all around them.

Arrows joined the bullets. Another horse went down, screaming in pain and agony. Gypsy fought the impulse to stop and take care of the horse, but there was no stopping. The pounding of hooves kept her glued to the black horse's back.

Gypsy noticed that Tavish was headed back toward the campsite. That would never work. They needed to steer their stolen herd toward the mountains. Three miles at least, she'd figured when she made the plan. The Indians would have to regroup and find them. The last thing Hank needed was to have them regrouping right behind them. She rode the black hard until she was in front of Tavish again, then began to steer the stampeded herd back toward the north. He looked like a wild Irish clansman until he realized what she was doing, then simply nodded and followed her lead. A bullet shot past his ear so close he could feel the heat from it, but he was still alive. By golly, they'd done it. They'd stolen all the horses, and now they'd only have to ride like the devil for a few miles, scatter them to seven ways to Sunday, and ride back to the campsite. With a little bit of Irish luck, they could sneak in and no one would ever be the wiser. Faith, but that Gypsy Rose Dulan was a piece of work who had the luck of the fairies riding with her.

The sting in her upper arm let Gypsy know her luck had played out. She glanced down long enough to see the blood running down her arm. Well, it would have to wait, she thought with light-headed fervor. They'd done it. She and Tavish had left a whole war party on foot back there. So she had taken a bullet. That didn't mean anything. Lots of people lived after they'd been shot she reminded herself as the raging pounding of more than four hundred hooves beat down on the earth all around her.

When they'd outrun the rage of bullets and arrows, and were well on their way to the far mountains, she laid forward, hugging the horse's neck with her good arm and laying her face in the soft, sweaty, silky mane. He'd done what she'd asked of him and she couldn't fault him for one of those hundreds of bullets finding a home in her arm. It had begun to burn like pure fire and the stars were blurring together into one big light, but she kept her eyes open, watching the freed ponies, running, sweat glistening on their bodies as they tasted the freedom they'd been born into.

Tavish reined in his big red horse. He hadn't ever ridden or expected so much out of a horse before but the big roan had come through. No doubt, if he decided to put the horse on the oval race track someday, it would be a winner. The ponies ran past him and Gypsy, tearing off in every direction. Some went toward the mountains in a flurry of hooves, the scent of hot, scared horse flesh going with them; others made a semi-circle and headed toward Colorado.

Tavish sat still for a few minutes, the heart of his horse still racing with the freedom he'd just experienced; beating almost as fast as Tavish's. A wide grin split his handsome face as he looked back to see Gypsy catching her breath, hugging her horse. Faith, but he'd never seen a woman ride like that before. After he gave her a piece of his mind for her crazy, senseless act, he intended to hear her story about just how those Mexican people did that. Jumping from one horse to another. Riding bareback as if it were the most natural thing in the world. The black was standing still, his head down, panting and Gypsy still didn't move.

"Aye, lassie, we did it. We've got two hours of riding to get us back to the camp, but maybe we can make it by daylight," Tavish said softly.

Gypsy heard a faint buzzing. Had Tavish made it or was he laying out there on the ground, trampled to death? She shuddered, the pain in her arm throbbing so badly by now that she could scarcely breath. Tavish. Dead? And she hadn't told him how she felt. He would have died without knowing. She opened her blue eyes wide. There was a movement off to her right but her sight was fixed firmly on the stars. Secret in the stars, she thought with a smile playing at the corners of her lovely face. The secret was that she loved Tavish. *"Te quiero,"* she mumbled in Spanish. Before she could say, "I love you," in English the stars twinkled one last time and blinked out, darkness filling her heart and soul.

Tavish reined in beside her just as she shut her eyes. "No more tricks, Gypsy Rose," he said harshly. "We've got a fight to have between here and the wagon train, and by faith we'll have it. So sit up and let's be on the way with the journey and the fighting, lass."

He reached out to touch her arm and brought back a fist full of sticky blood, black in his hand by the pale reflection of the stars. He jumped off his horse and caught her as she slid sideways into a heap of leather skirt, black hair and blood into his arms. With tears flowing down his cheeks, he laid her on the ground and checked her pulse, expecting to find nothing. A steady heartbeat and sturdy pulse surprised him. He ripped the sleeve of her shirt away from the bloody arm and found the bullet had cut deep into the upper muscle. He found both the small entry wound and the gaping, ragged exit one. Using the sleeve, he tied a tight tourniquet as high as he could.

He fixed the black's lead rope to his saddle horn and awkwardly mounted the big roan with Gypsy still in his arms. The idea of sneaking in and their stunt not being found out was out of the question. It was two hours back to the camp and infection could already be setting in. If she lived, her arm would be useless for a few weeks. A stone lay where his heart had been only hours before. He'd breathed in the still faint rose scent sneaking through the smell of fear, the sticky unmistakable odor of blood and all the other things that made up Gypsy. He held her tight against his chest, ignoring the wetness of the blood as it soaked the front of his shirt.

*"Taim i' ngra leat,"* he mumbled in Irish. "I love you," he said in English, tears dripping from his strong jaw and onto her black hair. Laying there like sparkling diamonds, glistening on the long black braids, the droplets of his salty tears spoke volumes. He'd been such a fool, avoiding her like she was the plague. Maybe if they'd been talking, she would have confided in him about her foolish plans and he could have talked her out of them. Or else taken her ideas to Hank. He and Bobby should have been the ones out there on that raid. He rode along at a steady pace, not trusting the big horse to run all the way back to the camp without dropping dead and yet wanting to race him so he could get help for her quicker. Both horses glistened with sweat covering their powerful bodies. Both of them more than content to walk at a steady pace.

He worried about Gypsy more than the horses, though. For a bit of her sassy tongue, he'd come close to putting a bullet through either horse, and he loved the big chestnut-colored roan as much as he'd ever loved anything or anyone. Until now. Although she sagged in his arms, he was grateful that her heart continued to beat in unison with his.

Two hearts.

Two souls.

Belonging together.

Yet could not.

The sun was barely a sliver of orange on the eastern horizon, giving forth a few rays to open up the new day, when he caught sight of the circled wagons. He held her close and kissed the top of her head for the hundredth time since he'd picked her up. "I'm so sorry, my love," he whispered. "You'll never know how much I love you, Gypsy Rose Dulan, because you are promised to the rich gold miner. But I'll know, and I'll remember the feel of you in my arms when I'm an old man."

He held up a hand and shouted when he was close enough to see the reflection of dozens of rifles pointed right at them. "Hey, don't shoot. It's Tavish. Don't shoot."

"What the devil?" Garnet said. "Is that Gypsy he's got all hugged up to him? I told you they'd run off together, Gussie. I told you."

"I reckon it is," Gussie smiled. "Looks like they didn't run very far though, did they?"

"Looks like they've both got a lot of explainin' to do, though, don't it?" Hank said coldly. "You women keep your rifles trained on the area in front of your wagon. Don't take them down until I say so."

Tavish rode right into the midst of them. The smile left Gussie's face when she looked up and saw the blood-stained shirt and her little sister's limp form. "What has happened. Is she alive?" She threw down a double hand full of ammunition and held out her arms for Tavish to hand Gypsy down to her.

"She's been shot," Tavish said. "Still alive and the bullet went in and came out but there's been a lot of blood. You better get her in the wagon."

"And you?" Hank noticed the blood on Tavish's shirt.

"I'm fine. Just fine. 'Tis her blood you'd be seein' Hank. I'll explain it all but could we get the wagons on the trail? We need to put some distance between us and that war party back there."

"That renegade war party is going to be bearing down on us any minute," Hank reminded him.

"Aye," he said. "They were. But they won't now. Not unless they'll be bearing down on you in their moccasins. They have no horses. They'll be spending the next week rounding up their mounts. By then we'll be through the pass on our way to Fort Bridger. So if these women could hitch up, it would be a good thing for us to be on our way. I don't know how fast they can run or if they'll want to attack on foot, but we should be going."

"You've got an explaining to do," Hank pointed at him. "Put the rifles away, ladies. Hitch 'em up. We'll pull out in ten minutes. One woman rides in the wagon with a loaded gun all day, though. Choose 'em up and let's go."

"Lord, Gussie, is she dead?" Garnet asked as Gussie laid her gently on the floor of the wagon.

"No, her heart still beats strong. But she's lost a lot of blood. Annie you take the driving. Merry, you ride close to her. Garnet you ride shotgun with a loaded gun. I'm going to see to Gypsy. Get me a basin of water and help me get her inside. Gypsy Rose, if you ever wake up, I'm going to kick you halfway back to Missouri."

Garnet pulled a silver flask of whiskey from her trunk and tossed it over to Gussie. "Brought it along in case we needed it. Clean it out with that, and wrap it with this after you stitch up that gaping hole where the bullet came out. She's going to be an old bear for a month," she said, tearing a long strip from a petticoat she jerked out of the trunk. "What she do, roll in the dirt? Look at her fingernails. When you get her gunshot taken care of, then you better give her a bath. And Gussie, you're going to have to stand in line to kick her into next week. I get to whip her soundly first just for scaring the liver out of us."

"I told you she hadn't been kidnapped by the Indians or run off with Tavish either," Gussie snorted. "If one had come within ten feet of her, she'd have slit his throat with that knife she carries. And she might love that Irish boy, but he's not the one in her dreams. She wants a tall, good-looking blond man with blue eyes. Not a short little cocky Irishman who raises her ire just being in her presence."

"Ain't that the truth. Honey, she wouldn't have that sorry Irish boy on a silver platter with an apple in his mouth. I'm not sure she'd like him if he was walking on the top of a barbed wire fence in his bare feet, singing her favorite song and bearing a bouquet of wild flowers," Garnet said, eyeing her sister as Gussie stripped away her shirt and assessed the wound.

"She'll live," Gussie said. "It's a clean shot. Give me that whiskey. I wish she was awake so she'd feel the pain. It would serve her right for what she's done. Whatever it is. Do you think she and Tavish took care of all those Indians single-handedly?"

Gypsy shuddered from her black braids down to the ends of her toes when Gussie poured the whiskey into the hole and it hit the raw flesh. She'd been engulfed in a great warm darkness when suddenly the most horrid pain snapped her back into the reality of living. It burned so bad she wanted to scream, but her voice was still in the darkness. She heard two of her sisters in the distance and they sounded angry. Was she dying and going toward Velvet? If so, why wasn't Velvet coming to meet her, to take her over the line into eternity?

"Okay, get up there on the seat with Annie," Gussie pointed.

"I'm staying right here. I'll keep an eye out the back of the wagon. If those Indians decide to attack now, it'll most like come from that way, so I'm staying. Besides even if they shoot flaming arrows into the wagons, I'm not going, Gussie. She's my sister too," Garnet said, propping the rifle against the wagon's tail gate. "Now hand me another rag and I'll start washing her up while you do the doctoring."

Between the two of them they had her clean and tucked into a makeshift bed on the floor of the wagon in an hour. By the time the sun rays were beating down, Gussie was outside, walking beside the wagon and Garnet was serving both as rifle-bearing sentinel and nursemaid to the sleeping Gypsy. The women kept close to the wagons, wary of what might still be coming any moment. Quietness replaced what was usually easy banter amongst them. No one talked of future husbands, when the future alone might be a miracle they would never see. Wariness floated above the whole train most of the morning, but by nooning, when nothing had happened, tension began to loosen up.

"What happened?" Gussie asked Tavish when they stopped for their midday meal of cold biscuits. No bean patties today. The women had prepared a quick breakfast in the dark, not knowing when or if they'd ever eat again, and then left in a hurry, so there'd been no time to fry up last night's beans into patties for the nooning.

"How is she?" he asked.

"Answer me first," Gussie demanded. "How could you let her get shot?"

"Me let her!" He threw up one hand. "Faith, Gussie Dulan, you should have seen her. It's a wonder she isn't dead, so many foolish chances she took. And all for the rest of you, for all of us." He raked his hand through his hair. "Please tell me if she's awake now. I've got a mad on that is going to take a whole lot of pure Irish screaming to get out of my system, and she's the one who is going to get screamed at."

"You'll not raise your voice to her, Tavish O'Leary. Not now. Not ever. You're going to leave her alone. This foolhardy stunt just proves that you aren't worthy of her even looking sideways at you," Gussie said.

"Aye, but I will have my say and it wasn't my foolhardy stunt, Gussie. It was hers. I barely got there in time to help her carry it out. If I could have carried her out on my back, I would have, but she'd already set the whole thing in motion when I arrived. It was do or die, with most of the betting on the die part. I still can't believe all those bullets and arrows didn't kill us both."

"Then have your say," Garnet poked her head out of the wagon sheet. "What went on out there?"

"She went sneaking out of camp. Took that big black spare horse. Rode out on it bareback. By the time I figured out it was her going out to the Indians, it was too late to do anything but mount up and follow her. She had a mind to stampede their horses. And there wasn't a thing I could do by the time I got there but help her. She let out a war whoop that probably is still ringing in them Indians' ears, and we rode like the devil was licking behind our ears for about three miles. She laid forward on that horse, like it was a blanket on the ground on a Sunday mornin' social after church, and drove those horses like she'd been born to do that job. Sometime along that time she took the bullet in the arm. By then we had them going the way we wanted them to go. Not that we cared, long as they were scattered seven ways to Sunday, but we didn't want them coming toward the wagon train. They headed north and some south. I talked to her, but she was already unconscious. I brought her back, and now I want to know how she is."

"She's sleeping, still," Garnet said. "I'd have gone with her just to see that sight."

"No, you don't want to see it or hear it. It'll give me nightmares for the rest of my life. It's a scary memory even yet. Aye, it is," he nodded seriously. "You'll take care of her, proper?"

"We are her sisters, Tavish O'Leary," Gussie said. "When she wakes up, she may tell us to come gunnin' for you for getting her shot."

"I didn't get her shot," he declared. "She all but got me killed, jumping from that Indian pony onto her horse like a fairy in the wind. When she wakes up tell her to show you how well she rides."

*If she wakes up,* he thought as he rode to the rear again, scanning their back trail, making sure the Indians weren't indeed following them on foot. *She might be a trick rider but she's still a delicate woman, and she's been through an ordeal the likes of not many women would ever live through even without a hole in her upper arm.*

*"Te quiero,"* she mumbled in her semi-consciousness. *"Te quiero."*

"What are you saying? What do you want?" Garnet bathed her face with a cool, wet cloth. "A drink of water.

Please don't get a fever with this, little sister. Just gripe and complain all you want, but live. Watching them take Velvet away to probably die was more than my heart could stand. To find a family and then lose it ain't right. You open them eyes and tell me what it is you're muttering in Mexican for. I'll get it for you if I have to move heaven, Hades and half the mountains in Arkansas. Just stay alive."

*I want Tavish O'Leary and I cannot have him,* Gypsy thought just before that warm darkness folded its arms around her again and rocked her soundly to sleep.

## *Chapter Ten*

"I want to see her," Tavish said as he met the formidable two sisters at the back of the wagon. "Is she awake, yet?"

"No, and you're not going inside that wagon." Gussie poked him in the chest with her forefinger. "She's restless enough as it is, talking in some Mexican language and tossing around. You'd agitate her even more. If she even sensed you were in the room, she'd get worse. You two just flat bring out the worst in each other."

"Maybe so, but I'm going in that wagon," Tavish said.

"Oh, Tavish, honey," Connie yelled from across the camp. "Come on over here and have a slice of cake with us. Bertie made a lovely cinnamon cake. We're making a pot of fresh coffee. We want to thank you proper for saving us from the Indians. Oh, when I think of what we almost endured I just get the pure old vapors."

"No, thanks," Tavish said bluntly. "I'm going in to check on Gypsy. If you want to thank someone, thank her. She's the one who saved a lot of bloodletting. I just got there in time to help out a little."

Connie threw her head back and stuck her nose straight up. It would be a cold day in July when she thanked one of those abominable Dulan sisters for a blessed thing. Tavish O'Leary was a fool for spending so much time with them, especially that half-breed Gypsy. Willow was a thorn to bear, but Gypsy, that woman was a pure cross. Connie hoped she had to marry some toothless old man with a bald head when they got to Bryte.

"You're not going in there," Gussie said again, tossing her long tawny-blond hair back over her shoulder. Soon it would be dry enough to put back up and get out of her face. Men didn't know how fortunate they were to be able to cut their hair all off above their ears, and not bother with it at all.

"Yes, Gussie, I am," Tavish threw back the wagon sheet and was inside before Gussie could grab him.

He might get around her with his quickness, but she'd be trussed up, rolled in molasses and staked out on top of an ant pile before she let him have time alone with Gypsy. Not even one minute. She stood beside the back of the wagon, her Dulan blue eyes boring holes in Tavish as he dropped down on his knees beside Gypsy.

Ignoring Gussie altogether, he took Gypsy's delicate hand in his, kissed the knuckles softly and murmured something in his Irish tongue that sounded so sweet to Gussie's ears—like the language butterflies would use if they could talk. The tone of his voice sure didn't sound like he was about to set up a war with Gussie's younger sister. If anything, it held under currents of great pain, bordering on feelings of pure love. He sat flat down on the floor of the wagon, his back pressed against trunks, and his legs curled under him. Being careful of her wounded wing, he gathered her into his arms, cradling her head against his chest and kissing her forehead. "I'm so sorry that you are hurting. *Taim i' ngra leat. Taim i' ngra leat.* Nothing can be done about it because fate already set the wheels in motion before I met you, lassie. But it doesn't change one thing about the way I feel. I will come back and tell you later. Aye, I will return, Gypsy Rose, and tell you again. Even though you can not ever return the feelings, I will tell you and then

I will go away and be content with the precious memories to keep me."

*Whisper more to me,* Gypsy thought in semi-consciousness. *Tell me those Irish words. I don't care what they mean. This feels so right—you holding me. Come back, Tavish, don't go away. Te quiero, my darling. I love you, even though it can not ever be possible to go further. Te quiero. Don't go. Keep me close to your heart. Hold me close. Talk to me more.*

Gussie had heard enough. Gypsy seemed content in her sleeping state and Tavish looked like he would sit there all night just holding her and murmuring words of comfort in her ears. Gussie sighed deeply as she went back to her chores. If she married at the end of this endless trail, she'd be more than grateful if it could be to a man who'd love her like that. Tears stung her eyes as she busied herself with the water barrel. Tavish O'Leary loved her sister, and she'd just witnessed the most touching scene in her entire life. Not even the sight of Willow standing up there in her pretty blue travel dress beside Rafe Pierce and vowing to love him until death would part them, not even that had touched Gussie like seeing the pain and anguish in Tavish O'Leary's black eyes as he kissed Gypsy's forehead.

"Well, what brought on those tears? Oh, Gussie, Gypsy didn't . . ." Garnet stumbled over the word, ". . . die?"

"No, she's fine, Garnet. It's just that . . ." Gussie dried her eyes on her apron tail.

"What?" Garnet demanded.

"She's going to live," Tavish said before Gussie could form her thoughts into mere words. "She's too stubborn to die. You're good doctors."

"We're her sisters. We love her," Garnet said.

"I'll be on my way now but I'll be back. I want to talk to her when she wakes," Tavish said. "Hank is over being mad, by the way. He's grateful to the she-cat in there for saving all our hides. By the time the story gets out, those

Indians are going to feel pretty foolish, that a woman defeated them."

"A woman and a man," Gussie drew herself up to her full five feet, eight inches, towering above Tavish. "She might not be in as good a shape as she is in there if you hadn't helped. So we'll give credit where it's due. She'll be awake by morning, surely."

"Thank you, Gussie," Tavish said tipping his hat.

"Now what brought that on? You were ready to kill him dead earlier and now you're treating him like a brother. Lord, I expected you to hug him there for a minute," Garnet said when he was out of hearing distance.

"He's in love with the imp," Gussie said, a smile twitching at the corners of her mouth. "Said he couldn't do a thing about it, but he's in love with her all the same. I don't want her to fall for him, Garnet. I want both of you to go on to California and live close to me forever."

"Well, that's her decision, ain't it?" Garnet swallowed down a lump the size of a Christmas orange in her throat. "But I'm telling you, you ain't got a thing to worry about. Two days and she'll be back breathing fire and spitting pure old meanness at one Tavish O'Leary. It was just the moment. They survived a frightful battle out there and they did it together and he held her, letting all that blood run all over him too. It's not love as in passion and forever amen; it's love as in we're alive and we won."

"I hope so Garnet. I hope so. When she wakes up and he goes in there to tell her he loves her, I hope she spits in his eye. Just like Willow did when Malachi Brubaker kept on pestering her to go to Utah with him and be his first wife."

"We lost Willow anyway, though, didn't we? And then Velvet too. Are we the only two who's going to see those gold miners, Gussie?"

"Can't answer that one."

It was late in the middle of the night when Gypsy opened her eyes and stifled a moan. A quick survey let her know she'd made it back to camp. She was in the wagon anyway. She tried to sit up but the first try was futile. Her arm throbbed. Her stomach growled. She'd been shot and she was starving to death. She moaned, not knowing which was worse. The pain tearing at her arm or the hunger ripping her stomach apart.

Gussie dozed under the wagon, snatching bits of sleep while she listened for her sister. When she heard the moan she threw back the sheet covering her and was beside Gypsy before her eyes were fully opened. "You awake, Gypsy?" she whispered, laying her hand on Gypsy's forehead, checking for fever.

"Yes," she said through a mouth drier than the desert sands in July. "And hungry."

"Girl, it's past midnight. But I reckon I could rustle up a bowl of cold beans or if you could wait, I could heat them up. Fire is still going out there. You remember anything?"

"Remember getting shot and thinking I'd died. How'd I get back here? Tavish? Oh my lord, is he dead?" Gypsy's blue eyes shot open, begging for answers.

"Tavish came hauling you in just after daylight. When we woke up and you were gone and he was, too, talk went around real quick that the two of you had run off in fear of the attack. Me and Garnet told them they were crazier'n outhouse rats. You running off with Tavish. Now that's not likely. Before we could hardly think about it, he was yelling out there for us not to shoot. You can be glad you was out cold. I poured whiskey in the gunshot and stitched up the exit hole. If you hadn't been stone dead to the world, you'd a raised a ruckus loud enough to scare the bedevil out of every Indian in the state."

"I'm hungry," Gypsy said again. "Cold beans are fine. Got a biscuit left?"

"I reckon I could rustle up a couple if you'll be still."

Gypsy tried to sit up again, this time with better results. The trunks in the wagon wiggled more than a little bit, but she got control of the light-headedness quickly. Strange, she thought she could detect a faint hint of Tavish O'Leary right there in the wagon beside her. She'd dreamed about him holding her, whispering love words in her ear in that soothing Irish tongue. He'd kissed her eyelids and said he would come back another time, but that was impossible. It had just been a dream. It couldn't be real. Tavish O'Leary didn't love Gypsy. Hate her would be the better word. He'd like to string her up from the nearest oak tree for her stunt, but it had worked. That which common sense had said couldn't be done, had been. Out of sheer determination and a little good old gypsy luck, she'd thwarted that raid, all right. But if there was going to be another one, someone else was going to have to step up and do their duty by the wagon train. She'd used up all her luck in the past 24 hours.

She sighed and touched the bandage covering her arm. Just the gentle pressure of her fingers sent it into a howling miserable fit. She'd have to make a sling or she'd never be able to walk 12 miles tomorrow. She grimaced just thinking about her arm hanging or worse yet, swinging as she kept pace with the oxen pulling the wagon. Tavish would have more than a few words to say when he found out she'd wakened up. He'd promised her a battle out there. Well, just because she had a wounded wing didn't mean she couldn't still speak her piece and tell him where he could go and how he could get there. She began to look forward to the fight. Maybe he'd bring it on before breakfast and she could work up another appetite.

Gussie gave a silent word of thanks that her sister was truly awake, alive and actually hungry. She dished up a bowl of lukewarm beans and crumbled a biscuit over the top. The coffee was strong enough to melt Gypsy's teeth, but it would probably taste good after having slept so long. Tomorrow would be plenty of time to alert Tavish that she was awake. He could tell her whatever he liked, and she could tell him to go all the way back to Ash Hollow and take a flying leap off the cliff, or forward to the nearest mountain and fly off it. At least, that's what Gussie hoped for. Garnet stirred in her sleep and opened her eyes as Gussie made her way back to the wagon. Gussie whispered that Gypsy was awake and hungry.

"Can I do anything?" Garnet asked.

"Got it under control. Go to sleep. You've got to drive tomorrow," Gussie said.

"Tell her I love her," Garnet said drowsily.

Gypsy ate her fill, chased Gussie back out to get some rest, and propped herself up at the back of the wagon. Could it really be that just 24 hours ago she'd ridden out and succeeded in what she went to do? The stars blinked brightly and one fell from heaven's glory as she watched. She couldn't make a wish. She was alive. That was enough of a marvel for one day.

*"Te quiero,"* she muttered. But for him to love her back, well that was too much of a miracle to ask for too. It was just the moment. Just a rush of feelings begging to be let out. Kiss me. Tell me I'm still alive. Tell me I'm not dead. I beat the Grim Reaper in this fight. Hold me. Let me feel your heart beating against mine so I'll know we are both alive.

Just the flow of life in their veins.

At least that's what she kept telling herself.

Tavish awoke with a start, the sound of Gypsy's war cries filling his ears, the sight of her on that big black horse, laid out on its back and sawing through the rope with that little *bodkin* she carried when the one horse went down. It took him a moment to still his heart and remind himself it was a dream. Reality had passed and what he'd just experienced was a dream born of it. He pulled his boots on and wandered toward the circle of wagons a few yards away. He'd just peep in the back of the wagon and make sure she was still breathing.

He scarcely breathed as he slid his leg over the wagon tongue and pulled back the dusty wagon sheet. Startled out of his mind when he found her sitting there staring at him, he couldn't control the way his body jumped. His heart raced at the sight of her in her snowy-white night rail buttoned up the neck, a rusty spot of dried blood on one of the sleeves. Her skin was as pale as the dim light but she was sitting up, staring right at him as if he was a ghost.

"You scared the liver out of me," she whispered.

"Well, you took five years off my life," he whispered back. "Can I come in there with you?"

"Ruin your reputation for sure," she said.

"Aye, but it's already ruined," he said, hefting his weight into the wagon beside her.

For a long time they sat quietly, trying to form wordless emotions into expressions to describe their feelings. Him, trying to get the courage to tell her how he felt and how he shouldn't. Her, still letting the surge of life flow through her body and soul in gratitude that they were still connected.

"You promised me a fight because of what I did," she said after a while. "I'm too tired to fight tonight so if that's what you've come for . . ."

He bracketed her lovely mouth by placing his palms on her delicate cheeks, then he leaned forward and claimed it for his own. Even if it was just for a brief instant, it was his for that time. He tasted sweetness, courage and love surrounded by the sweet smell of rose water. She tasted gentleness, bravery and fearlessness and wanted to live forever with her eyes closed and Tavish O'Leary's mouth glued to hers.

*"Taim i' ngra leat,"* he whispered. "That means I love you in Gaelic, Gypsy Rose Dulan. And I do love you. I love your zest for life. I love you because you don't think of tomorrow and you live for today. I love you for all those reasons and more. But I cannot love you. You are promised to another man. To one who's bought and paid your passage. I'll have to make do with my precious memories. No, don't say a word. Don't tell me to go shoot myself between the eyes so the nonsense can pour out of my poor feverish

brain. I do love you, but I do not intend to do one thing about it. I will stay away from you and will never put you in danger again."

"You didn't put me in danger. I put me there," she said. Where was this conversation going anyway? He loved her. He didn't love her? The stupid Irish pig. If he loved her, he'd do anything to convince her to be his wife. All he could do was talk in riddles and spout off Irish blarney. That probably meant he didn't love her at all. It was probably a curse he'd put on her to cause her to never love anyone else.

"Aye, but that was your body. Your heart must belong to someone else," he said.

"You Irish! You always love to be a martyr," she hissed.

"Aye, you are going to live. You are back to your old self, already," he flashed her a grin that took her breath away.

She reached out, wrapped her one good arm around his neck and brought his lips to hers for another kiss. She understood. He'd said those words to her when she was bleeding on his shirt—in the rush of the moment. Now he had to explain them away. Well, she understood all too well. He might have loved her then. He might even love her now, but there was no way he would ever take a half-breed Mexican home to meet his lace-curtain Irish family.

He'd saved her life by carrying her back to her sisters. She would be grateful for that and hold his handsome face in her heart forever. When she was an old woman, she'd sit on Gussie's front porch and remember the way the stars paled in comparison to the sizzling sparks dancing around them when their lips touched. She'd never marry; not ever. All she'd have to offer a man would be a heartless shell of what used to be a sassy woman.

Out of pure gratitude, she'd let him keep his pride. "Get out of here, you little Irish boy, and stop telling me such nonsense. We both know they were only words spoken in the heat of the battle. We were alive and we had outwitted a whole tribe of fierce Indians. Go back to your camp and get some sleep. And quit saying you love me. We'll fight later. Now, I'm tired and want to sleep, Tavish O'Leary."

"Goodnight," he swallowed the lump in his throat. She didn't love him. She couldn't anyway. She'd come from gentry, albeit Mexican, but still wealthy gentry. His family had clawed its way up from poor Irish farmers in the old country, coming through Irish gypsies in the eastern part of the states, to where they were today in Utah. They'd moved west when they saved enough money, and years later, with hard work, blood and sweat they'd begun the horse operation in Utah. She'd never be happy in a little two-room cabin. Not Maria Marguerite Gypsy Rose Dulan. She deserved crystal and mansions. Not log cabins and smoky lanterns. She should sit on a pedestal that reached halfway to heaven itself. He could never offer anything but a poor little Irish heart full of love. And she'd just let him know that wouldn't be nearly enough for her.

He slung a leg out of the wagon and didn't even look back. If he had, he would have seen a single tear cutting the pathway for a million more flowing over the dam behind those pretty blue eyes. If his heart hadn't been pounding so hard with disappointment he would have heard her say ever so softly, "*Te quiero,* my darling."

## *Chapter Eleven*

Gypsy loved her sisters, she really did. But if they didn't quit smothering her, she swore she was going to drown herself or them the next chance she got. Gussie would have chewed her food for her if she'd but asked. And Garnet hovered around like a mother hen. Gypsy expected to hear her begin a clucking noise any moment.

As if that weren't enough, women kept stopping by the wagon the next night, asking if she needed anything. Guilt washed over her every time someone said or did something nice, but the trapped, I-can't-breath feeling was stronger than the guilt. In 24 hours, she'd lived too much and too hard. She needed time to sort through it. Time alone. Time to come to terms with having walked down that shadow of death and come out the other side still alive.

Two people had carefully steered clear of her all day. Connie was still in a royal blue-blooded pout that would probably last all the way to California. Gypsy hoped when they got there, the man Connie married lived so far outside of town that they only came around once a year. And Tavish had stayed true to his word. He'd ridden far enough at the rear of the wagon train that she could feel his eyes on her that morning when she did walk for a couple of hours before she had to crawl back into the wagon and rest. Both of them were nowhere to be seen. Idly, Gypsy wondered if they were together. If Tavish had decided that the whining, clinging Connie would be an angel straight from the puffy clouds compared to the impetuous Gypsy, who didn't have a lick of common sense. Gypsy turned a light shade of green at the idea of him kissing Connie, then shrugged it off. After all, who he did or did not kiss wasn't one bit of her business, and besides, she'd give them her blessings if she could have even half an hour of time to herself.

*Yeah, right*, she thought. *And who's kidding who, Gypsy Rose Dulan? You've got yourself in a fine pickle. The one you want, won't have you. You don't want him to say he loves you because it hurts too bad to hear it and not have the future that goes with it. You'll have to do what you've been doing to maintain your dignity and your sanity. Just stay away from him, like you've done all day.*

At nooning, Tavish had joined them for Annie's bean patties, biscuits stuffed with the last of some venison Bobby shot and shared amongst all the women. He had carefully avoided her eyes, and even when her fingers had brushed against his as she'd handed him a second bean pattie, he hadn't looked up with a smoldering look in his dark eyes like he usually did. She'd endured the burning sensation in her fingers in solitude.

He'd disappeared to the men's camp when the train stopped for the day at Sublette Cutoff. The trail forked about a mile back; one bearing off slightly to the north, mostly to the west; the other south and west. Gypsy had heard the men talking about that northern route. It would cut off three days travel in the long run, but it required a waterless drive across a barren desert between the Big Sandy and Green Rivers, followed by the necessity to climb several mountainous ridges west of the Green River. She hoped if those angry Indians had rounded up their horses by now and were in hot pursuit with revenge on their minds, that they took the wrong route and poisonous lizards attacked them. She'd wish a worse curse on them for shooting her in the arm, but she didn't have a minute to herself to conjure one.

Just before she began to bite at her sisters and the rest of the wellwishers, she made an excuse to go outside the camp to find a bush. "I'll only be a few minutes," she said.

"I'll go with you. You might need some help." Garnet laid down the paring knife and wiped her hands.

"If you take one step with me, I intend to use my good hand and yank your hair all out by the roots," Gypsy said, no smile on her face and not a hint of humor in her voice. "If I don't get out of all this chattering and noise, I'm going to start screaming and throwing things."

"Well, what jumped up and bit you on the rear end? Everyone is just trying to be nice."

"Noise. Confusion. People. If I don't have a half an hour by myself, I'm going to start foaming at the mouth."

"Then you ain't needin' a bush for nature?" Garnet asked, her own eyes glittering with merriment.

"No, I'm not. So there. I've just got to have some time to get my thoughts and mind together. I can't even breathe."

"See you in thirty minutes," Garnet said. Her sister was truly going to live through this after all. Whether or not she and Tavish admitted what the whole train could see was their business. The tension between them was so thick at nooning that it couldn't have been cut through with that dagger Gypsy carried around in her skirt tail. Watching people fall in love sure wasn't easy on Garnet. Each day brought her closer and closer to the end of the journey where she'd have to stand up beside a man and promise to marry him. Each day the fear of doing just that caused her stomach to knot up in pure agony. Thinking back about Rafe and Willow and the love they shared, and now Tavish and Gypsy, solidified Garnet's resolve that she wouldn't marry a man whose name she drew from a hat. If she couldn't have a romance, complete with all the heart-clenching pain of falling in love, then by golly, she wouldn't have any of it.

Gypsy adjusted the sling made from a pillow case, and breathed in the night air. The evenings had begun to get a little cooler, but then they should. August was almost gone now. It wouldn't be long until fall pushed summer into history and then it would just be a short slide into winter. By then the second of her adventures would be finished. Paqui said the first man wouldn't tell her what she wanted to hear; the second would tell her and she wouldn't want to hear it.

Well, that was the gospel according to an old gypsy woman she decided, as she sat down beside the quiet waters of the river with a lonesome bird singing in a sweet high voice. Jake Dulan was dead when she arrived in St. Joseph so there was no way he could tell her he loved her. And that's what she wanted to hear him say. Not even the words on the paper when Rafe read the will were a substitute for hearing him say it. Then the next adventure began and lo and behold, Tavish said he loved her, even though he didn't intend to do one thing about it. And she didn't want to hear it. Seeing him ride away to his Chalk Creek, Utah, home was going to rip her heart out. Knowing that he loved her would sear her soul forever.

"Evenin'," he said, throwing himself down beside her but keeping a healthy distance.

"What are you doin' out here?"

"Had to get away from it all for a while. Same as you."

"You said you'd stay away from me," she said.

"Is that what you want, Gypsy?"

"What I want hasn't been considered."

"What does that mean?" He raised an eyebrow over eyes as dark as a raven's feather.

"Where did you get those black eyes?" she asked, changing the subject. What good did it do to hash through the whole thing again? He'd stated his position even though it wasn't the real reason he couldn't acknowledge his love for her.

"From my maternal grandmother."

"Irish have blue eyes. Red hair and blue eyes."

"Some of them do. I'm the apple of my granny's eye, though because I got something that wasn't Irish."

"Oh, you have some mixture back there then?"

"Sure, my Da is Irish. Pure. Red hair, blue eyes. The whole thing like you said. So is his mother. His Da had the dark hair, but the blue eyes. Granda came over here on the boat from Ireland. He met and fell in love with Gran, who has the black hair and eyes so dark they really do look black."

Tavish was uncomfortable telling her about his family. Folks that knew him in Chalk Creek knew his family. People on the wagon trains he'd worked weren't interested in what part of the family tree got shook to make him have dark eyes. Sharing the history seemed to be taking a step in the wrong direction. She already thought him unsuitable for anything more than a quick kiss. Knowing the background he came from would seal that up tight.

"So where did she get dark eyes?" Gypsy asked, her curiosity piqued.

"You mentioned Paqui, the gypsy woman who comes to south Texas in the spring and helps with your horses?" He looked at her. Really looked at her, trying to drink in every little feature so he could remember it forever. Aye, but she was a beauty with her light coffee-colored skin, those mesmerizing blue eyes and all that flowing black hair.

"Are you evading this issue? Lord, I don't need to know your history from the sixth day of creation, Tavish. I just asked where you got those dark eyes."

"So we don't have to face the real issues, huh, Gypsy Rose Dulan? But I'll go back that far to tell you about my eyes because I have to start at the beginning," he chuckled. "My Granda worked in New York for a couple of years and saved every dime. He knew horses. I mean he really knew them. He can still sweet talk a horse into doing about anything for him. Then a big time southern horse man took a shine to him and offered him a job in South Carolina. From there, he went to Kentucky and wound up in Utah where he bought his own operation. He was in his thirties by then and he built his house with his own hands and logs from his ranch. Late one fall, the gypsies came and he hired them to help him do the chores through the winter months. Gran was a twenty-year-old beauty with black eyes and hair and Granda fell for her. They were married that next spring before her family went south again. Granda said he worried for years that the gypsy in her blood would take her from him. But she settled right into the ranch. She's about as smart when it comes to horses as Granda is. Paqui is her distant cousin, Gypsy. That's where I got the black eyes and I guess it makes me only three-fourths Irish and a quarter gypsy."

Gypsy could scarcely believe her ears. Talk about the world being a small place.

"Then they had a half a dozen kids. Four boys with Granda's red hair and blue eyes. Two daughters with Gran's dark hair but with the blue eyes. One of those boys, Morgan, is my Da. Mother is a full-blooded lace-curtain Irish lady. The prettiest chestnut hair you've ever seen even though it's got a gray one here and there to ice it now. I'm a throwback. My two older brothers are tall, light-haired and eyed. My two younger ones are already taller then me. Aye, even my two sisters are taller than I am. But I'm Gran's special baby because I'm short like her and my eyes are dark."

"I see," she said. So it wasn't because she was a mixed breed that he wouldn't allow himself to fall in love with her. It wasn't because he'd be ashamed to take her home to his family. It must be that he had a dream in his mind of who he would love, and he was willing to toss his bets on the ground and wait for her to come along. Gypsy could understand that but he should be honest about it. She'd wanted a tall, blond husband with blue eyes and a wickedly cute smile. Evidently, he surely did not want a short little woman with blue eyes and black hair. Or, most likely, one with a sassy attitude and was able to think for herself. Like all men she'd known, he'd want one of those simpering women, blond or dark, who fainted at the sight of blood, and clung to him like a fly on a cow chip. Yes, that was it. Gypsy was far too independent for the likes of Tavish. She set her jaw in determination not to change for any man. Whoever married her would just have to accept the whole package. Independence and all.

"So how's the arm?" he asked when the silence became deafening. "We still haven't had that discussion about your stupidity in running off like that."

"Stupidity!" She shouted all her frustrations out in one word.

"Aye, even though it might've saved lives, it was a stupid move."

"Might have!" she yelled again. "Might have! It was a wonderful plan and it worked. And it did save a lot of lives."

"But it wouldn't have if those Indians hadn't been wiped out from smoking that vision weed. If they'd been alert, they'd have spotted you. Those two guards almost found you. Didn't you see them scanning the brush?"

"I saw them," she said, her arm suddenly aching worse than it ever had. The audacity of him. The pure ego he pushed around in front of his handsome face. Both were going to trip him up one of these days. She pushed back the urge to slap thunder out of that same good-looking face. "I could've taken them out if I had to. I'm not a coward." She didn't believe her own boasting, though, as she remembered how much the idea of shooting a man, even a charging Indian, had affected her.

"Darlin', anyone who would think you a coward would have corn mush for brains. Your idea was wonderful and smart. The idea that you went off by yourself, a woman at that, is what is stupid."

She started to jump up and found it impossible to do with one arm. Unbalanced, she found herself tangled in her skirts and was well on her way to falling when Tavish's strong arms pulled her to his chest. The beating of his heart told her that she'd scared him as badly as she'd scared her ownself.

He tipped back her chin with his callused palm and bent ever so slightly to kiss those sweet lips. Just once more, he told himself just before that wonderful warm feeling invaded his body and the sizzle of desire shot through his veins. Just this once more and then he'd never put himself in the position to let it happen again.

Physical attraction, she told herself when he pulled back from the kiss and set her on solid ground. Nothing more. Even Connie could see a handsome man in Tavish O'Leary. That and the lilt of the Irish still in his voice even after three generations. Add his sparkling humor and wit, and who wouldn't be attracted to him? But she'd get over that in short order, she promised herself.

"I'm still not stupid," she said, a bit weakly.

"Aye, but the stunt you pulled was," he said. He'd walked away into the darkness by the time she realized he'd just had the last word.

She stomped the ground hard enough to put a fresh flash of pain all the way up her body to her sore arm. "You rotten Irish clod," she fumed all the way back to camp.

"So you get yourself a breath of fresh air or you ready to yank all my hair out?" Garnet asked when she spotted her storming across through the brush. The set of her jaw, the way her coal-black eyebrows knit together in a straight line both told Garnet that she hauled a worse mood back than she'd taken out.

"I'm ready to blow the bottom out of that commandment what says, 'Thou shalt not kill.' I'm not sure God was talking about the Irish, though. I think maybe he'd look the other way and maybe even wink if I shot an Irishman dead as a chunk of wagon iron."

"Tavish?" Gussie looked up from a mending job she was doing by the dim light of a dying campfire. "You in love with him?"

"Love him? I'd like to be the first one to throw the dirt in a six-foot hole over his wooden casket," Gypsy all but snorted.

"Drivin' you insane, is he?" Annie asked.

*"A que sí!"*

"Speak in English, not Mexican," Gussie said.

"That's not Spanish. It is gypsy for 'Isn't it so,' " she said. "That little Irish boy is about to drive me insane. Telling me I was stupid for saving the whole train from a massacre."

"And he's still alive?" Garnet asked. "He called you stupid. You've got a knife in your skirt tail and you let him live. Lord, girl, I do believe you do love him a little bit."

"Wouldn't do me a bit of good to love that rascal," Gypsy sighed. "He spouts a lot of blarney but he's got a whole 'nother idea of what kind of woman he wants to spend his life with. And dear sisters, it ain't a half-Mex with dark hair and misplaced blue eyes. Or one who can stand up and speak her mind, either. He's just another man who wants to feel big by having a simpering female stuck to his arm. Short men!"

"What about short men?" Annie asked.

"They're all full of themselves. All boisterous and opinionated. Just trying to make up for the fact they aren't real men. Never seen a short man yet that wasn't trying to prove something. And I've seen lots of them in the part of the world I was raised up in," she said. "Falling for a short man would be like signing your own death warrant. You'd have to walk two steps behind him and be treated like a prize puppy instead of a woman with a thinking mind."

"Besides you'd have to buy back your passage from Hank if you did decide to go with him," Annie said.

"Willow didn't have to," Gypsy said, incredulously. The idea that she couldn't just walk away had never occurred to her. She was her own person; a grown woman. But she had put her name on the line saying that when she reached Bryte, California she'd be willing to marry a man she'd never met. The reality of what she had done so carelessly suddenly made her shiver.

"Yes, but we still had several extra women," Annie reminded her. "And Rafe is Hank's good friend. Will be his neighbor when this run is over. That was a bit of a different story. Now we've lost two more women. The one we buried back there who died with the fever and Velvet. Hank's going to have to be careful not to lose any when we start across that big desert."

"You think he'd really make me pay him to let me go?" Gypsy asked. She had money in her trunk. Probably more than enough, and besides, Hank could recruit more women at Fort Bridger . . . maybe.

"You'd have to ask him," Garnet said.

"Well, we won't have to worry about that, will we?" Gypsy said coldly.

She slept poorly that night, her thoughts and arm both vying for attention and keeping her awake. Unable to sleep, she arose early and one-handedly had breakfast started when the rest of the women began to stir. Annie poured a cup of coffee and fussed at her. Garnet still hated to get up early after years of working half the night playing a piano in a saloon, and sleeping until noon, so she was grateful to have the coffee already brewed and ready. Gussie simply smiled. Her sister had a legion of emotional demons to do heart-to-heart battle with and no one could help her.

Gypsy managed to keep walking all morning that day. That was her goal. Even if she was worn out by dinner time and had to spend part of the afternoon in the wagon, she wanted to keep at it as long as she could. The last hour she really had to push herself, but she wouldn't let Tavish O'Leary see her stagger and fall.

They had their nooning beside a small cemetery. Six graves there in the middle of nowhere. With her good hand Gypsy picked a handful of wild flowers and placed one on each grave. The living honoring the dead, she thought as she read the carving on each of the wooden crosses. A family of four died right here just two years ago on their way to the promised land. A husband who'd had a better life in his eyes; a wife, who went with her husband to chase his dreams; two little boys, three and five, who didn't even have a choice. Did they run and play like Merry did? Did the people cherish their laughter and kiss their sweaty little faces at night? Gypsy hoped so. She hoped they had two good parents who loved them. By the dates, a 70-year-old man with a different last name died the day after the family did. Was he the wife's father? she wondered. And a 20-year-old fellow with the same last name as the old man. Her brother or a cousin perhaps? What a day it would have been in heaven. An old angel arriving. Baby ones. A sweet young couple which was so much in love and would never have to face life without the other one.

Death had respect for nobody. It had taken six lives and made them equal. She bowed her head in the heat of the day and in that moment forgave Jake Dulan for dying. He had no power over death. Neither would she when her time came. Someday the spirits of Jake and his daughter, Gypsy Rose, might sit down and get to know each other. They'd have all of eternity to do so. Someday she was going back to St. Joseph and put flowers on her father's grave. She'd have to tell the sisters. All five of them would meet there in St. Joseph someday. They'd pay their respects and let him rest in peace.

"That was a nice gesture," Tavish said so close behind her she could feel the heat from him radiating toward her heart. "But it's time to head 'em out again."

She wiped the tears from her eyes with her good arm and wordlessly brushed past him as she walked back to her sisters. If he had it in mind to avoid her, then she could darn well return the favor. She hoped his nerves quivered as much as hers did at just the touch of his skin on hers. And she hoped that tall blond with downcast eyes, and a whiny voice, the one she figured he had in mind to marry someday, served him up a lifetime platter of misery.

Tavish rubbed his arm where she'd touched him. Seemed almost like she'd done that on purpose. Didn't she know that even the most devout love in the world couldn't stand what they'd put it through? Besides, he was determined to fall out of love just as easily as he'd fallen into it. Faith and saints, he'd managed to get over the cholera when he was a teenager. He'd flirted with death for days and lived. This couldn't be any worse than that.

## *Chapter Twelve*

Gypsy sat on the banks of the Green River all day and watched the ferry take one wagon at a time. Hank, Bobby, Tavish and the rest of the hired hands drove each wagon's livestock to the other side, then came back to start all over again. Eight dollars was the price for every wagon that oversized crate transported, along with the women assigned to it. It was the most exorbitant thing she'd ever heard of. Eight dollars could keep a family in flour and supplies that couldn't be grown in the garden for weeks. Eight times 22 was too much money to think about spending in one day just to get from one side of the river to the other. Mr. Lombard who owned the ferry business no doubt was one very rich man.

And so were the men who'd paid to have wives brought to them. Gypsy began to count up expenses since they'd left St. Joseph, Missouri. The cost was staggering. Not even with the cache she had sewn into a velvet bag in her trunk could she ever buy back her freedom. Right now she was little more than one of the slaves in the southern states. She'd been bought and paid for. Someone else owned her and she'd signed her own name giving them permission to own her.

An afternoon breeze picked up the smoke from the

campfires on the other side where the women began to set up temporary housekeeping early. It blew across the river and stung Gypsy's eyes, but the tears flowing down her cheeks washed it away quickly. She watched them carry laundry down to the grassy edge of the calm waters and begin to wash. No doubt, they'd love to frolic in the water themselves since they had the whole of the afternoon and evening, but decorum even on the trail wouldn't let them shuck out of their clothing and jump into the cool water with the ferryman's eyes on them.

Sun rays filtered down through the gathering clouds, in a stream of magic, looking for all the world like a bolt of shimmering gossamer let loose to fall from heaven to earth. Gypsy slapped at mosquitoes and waited her turn to ride across the wide river on the ferry. Connie's and Bertie's wagon was next and then hers and it would be finished. She hoisted herself to her feet in time to see Connie sling herself around in a fitful tantrum and come stomping away from the ferry. Now what had set her off this time? Had Tavish refused to comfort her when a mosquito bit her on her pretty little neck?

"Looks like the ferry has shut down business for the night," Gussie said not far behind Gypsy.

"You mean, he's not going to take us all across?" Gypsy hadn't even thought of that concept. She just figured even if they went over in the dark they'd circle up the wagons and spend the night together like always.

"Oh, no!" she moaned as loud as Connie. "The last time we got stuck on one side of the river, remember what happened?"

"Yep, Rafe fell into the river and Willow had to jump in and save him. Then she took the rest of the wagons on ahead," Garnet said with a sly grin. "You going to jump in and save Tavish if he falls in the river?"

"No, I am not. If he can't swim the crocodiles can eat him. Of course, then we'll have to scoop up dead crocodiles because Irish meat will kill them. And I've told you two time and time again. History might repeat itself in war and rumors of wars, but it ain't repeating itself where Tavish and I are concerned. Rafe and Willow were made for each other. From day one, the sparks flew around them like lightning bolts. They just had to fall in love and admit it. Tavish O'Leary is a hard-headed Irishman that no self-respecting, independent woman would ever want. Besides all of which, he doesn't want a Mexican woman who reminds him of a squaw."

"Okay, okay. Besides, there ain't no crocodiles in the Green River. You'd just have to let the perch and catfish have him," Gussie laughed. "We got to keep each other company tonight along with Connie and her wagon full of women. That's enough to choke us all, so we won't talk about the Tavish thing. We might as well use the campfire pits left by the last bunch who didn't make it over in a day, and get some supper started. If we got dirty clothes we should take care of them too. Never know when the water holes will dry up and we'll be down to drinking and cooking water again."

Gypsy was glad for the subject change. Even more so when she realized Tavish O'Leary and Bobby were the ones assigned to stay on the side of the river with the last two wagons. She busied herself finding fuel to start a fire. She filled the pit closest to her wagon with small sticks, and when the blaze took hold, fed it with larger limbs. Bobby slid two big logs across the flames, making a stove top of sorts.

"We'd be obliged, Tavish and I, if we could share your supper," he said.

"Oh, Annie," Bertie yelled from the back of the other wagon, "would it be all right if we combined the supper tonight? We could make a pot of stew big enough for us all and help with the cleanup."

Annie looked at Gypsy, who shrugged in agreement even though she wanted to throw a stick of firewood at Bertie for even suggesting the idea. She'd rather share her supper with a rabid skunk than Connie. And in the presence of Tavish, to boot. Lord, the night would take forever to pass, with Connie's snide remarks flaring Gypsy's anger out of control; and Tavish's mere presence, blowing flames on the desire deep in her belly. Some days started off bad and just got worse as they wore on; this was one of them.

Gypsy wished for a long soak in a real bathtub with rose-scented soap as she watched Annie, Gussie and Garnet, along with Bertie and the other women from that wagon, share duties around the supper-fixing. Merry chased fireflies on the green grass between the wagons and the river. Bobby and Tavish took care of the oxen and horses, rubbing down their own mounts slowly and deliberately. Gypsy watched it all from her perch at the back of her wagon.

A woman could tell a lot about a man by the way he took care of his stock. Tavish's tack was always in good repair; the leather soft with regular applications of saddle soap, the iron cleaned with no visible rust. He spoke loving words to the horse as he gave him a thorough brushing, something he didn't often have the time to linger over at the end of the day. Would he be that gentle with the woman he spent his life with? She wondered.

"Hey, Uncle Tavish, look at all the fireflies I caught. It looks like a regular lantern in there," Merry said as she held up a quart fruit jar full of glittering bugs.

One of nature's many miracles, Gypsy thought. A bug that can turn its tail on and off as it flies through the skies. Not totally unlike Tavish, who could say he loved her but he wasn't going to admit it to his heart. Turn it on. Turn it off. Too bad he wasn't a firefly in that jar of Merry's. Well, she was going to turn it off and forget he'd ever said those sweet words, or that he'd kissed her either.

She forced her thoughts back toward a long bath. She imagined a long, oval tub filled with warm water, topped off by a layer of rose-scented bubbles. She inhaled deeply, but the only thing she caught a whiff of was the sweat she'd produced all day. Dark circles were still defined under her arms, as well as a big splotch right in the middle of her back. What kind of men would want to eat supper with nine sweaty women and one little girl? They must really be hungry.

Connie stepped into the light of the camp just as Tavish and Bobby strolled up and found a seat. Gypsy could've sworn the woman kept an eye peeled so she could make a dramatic entrance. The aroma of lemon followed her into the circle; her hair had been combed into an upsweep of golden-blond curls, and she wore a lovely pale-blue dress embellished with lace around the collar and sleeves. She'd pinched her cheeks until they were rosy, and a lovely smile covered her face.

*One for old Connie,* Gypsy thought as she looked down at her own hair, in a simple braid because it was easier for Gussie to fix that way in the rush of the mornings. Her dress, even minus the sweat stains, was calico faded by days and days of sun beating down on it, and nights and nights of washing in the plain old river waters. Her arm was in a sling and she couldn't have sashayed like Connie, swinging her hips provocatively as she ignored Gypsy and kept her big round clear-blue eyes on Tavish. No sir, if she'd tried to walk like that she'd have ended up sprawled out over the top of the campfire like a roasting piglet.

A man would have to be half blind, stone cold dead, and totally ignorant not to appreciate something that lovely after days and days on the trail. Tavish looked up and the look that went across his face was anything but a flash of desire. To Gypsy, he looked like he wanted to give the illustrious beauty an Irish dressing down for wasting precious time on making herself gorgeous when all the other women were busy taking care of survival. Gypsy could have fallen in his arms and kissed him until they were both breathless for that one look.

"Oh, Tavish, I thought maybe I'd just dress up for the

evening. You know, it's been hard to look so dowdy every day," Connie said as she cut her eyes around toward Gypsy.

"Well, you do look lovely," Bobby said with only a hint of humor in his voice. "I surely do hope that you don't get your dress all dirty when it's your turn to wash dishes, though. I'd bet that's the dress you're keeping back for the big wedding day at the end of the trip."

"Dishes?" Connie threw back her head, both flirty and feminine. "Darlin' I'm not doin' dishes tonight. Tonight I'm being pampered. Bertie is taking my place. I promised her I'd do them for a week, if I could just feel like a princess tonight. Lord, I'm so tired of dirt, dust and the smell of oxen, I could scream."

"Well, that's what you have to put up with to get the prize at the end," Bobby said. "A husband who'll let you wear pretty dresses at the supper table. Of course, you'll be expected to cook the supper and do the dishes afterward."

"My husband is going to be the richest man there," Connie said. She arranged her full skirt in a flowing sweep when she sat down on a rock. "I'm going to have a maid and maybe even a butler."

Bobby laughed. "You ever been to a gold mining town?"

"Of course not," Connie held her chin just so and looked down her nose at the Indian guide. She hadn't dressed up for him, and yet there he was doing all the talking while Tavish kept sneaking looks over at Gypsy. Well, after tonight he wouldn't look at her again. Lord, just look at her. Sweat circles under her arms and looking like she'd been the loser in a dirt-throwing contest. He was making some very careful comparisons, Connie just knew it in her heart. No, she wouldn't think of running away to marry the short little smarty pants Irishman, but by golly she'd make him think she would. Just so she could get back at Gypsy Dulan. Granted, she didn't like Gypsy and her courage, but she really hated Willow Dulan, who'd stolen Rafe from right under her nose. And for that, she'd get even with Gypsy.

At least she'd have a little bit of revenge on that Dulan bunch of sisters by making Tavish fall in love with her, and then sending him on his way.

Women like Connie had about as much brain power as an armadillo, Gypsy thought as she watched Connie flirt shamelessly, and the grins on Bobby's and Tavish's face as she flicked a little lace fan around, twittering and giggling behind it. One moment Gypsy was sure that they were barely tolerating the nonsense. The next she wondered if they weren't actually enjoying it. Even in her younger days when she first put on long skirts and put her hair up, she hadn't acted like that. Matter of fact, if she had to become a total idiot to get a man to notice her, then she'd go unnoticed.

Women were so silly, Tavish thought, seeing Connie make a complete fool of herself. Mercy, a prairie dog had more sense than that. The woman didn't have anything of substance between those big blue eyes or she'd know a man might be attracted to a pretty dress, a high pitched giggle and the nice clean smell of lemon, but a real man wanted a woman who could talk about more than the latest fashions.

"Well, Queen Connie," Annie said with more than a little sarcasm. "I expect you can be the first in line to help your bowl full of this stew. If you want to feel like a princess and if Bertie is willing to do dishes for you, that's all fine and good. But, I for one, am not scooping up your supper, young lady."

Gypsy saw the spiteful look Connie threw at Annie. Queen Connie: How fitting! The idea was born in the space of a moment, just like the one when she stole the horse and rode to the Indian's campsite. A smile tickled the corners of her mouth as she stepped up to the stew pot. "I'll help the queen's bowl tonight," Gypsy said: "Please your majesty, allow me. I'll serve you tonight. After all, I can never be as regal as you are. I'm just a squaw with a broken wing."

Connie smiled beautifully. Gypsy was certainly learning her place in a hurry. All it had taken was someone with the grace and knowhow to show her just how dowdy and unacceptable she was. But somehow, when she took the bowl of steaming soup from Gypsy's good arm, she didn't feel nearly so much that she'd won a victory, but that she'd been made a fool of.

Tavish almost choked on his own chuckle, but he kept it tucked away in his chest. Gypsy would never know how beautiful she was right at that moment. Putting Connie in her place so adeptly the girl didn't even know she'd been taken down a notch. Even in her faded dress and with the braid swinging down her back, Gypsy was far lovelier than the trussed up Connie. His hands, wrapped by now around a warm bowl of stew, rich with potatoes and carrots and venison broth, wanted nothing more than to throw it in the dirt and grab Gypsy as she passed by him on her way to refill her own bowl. To take the three sections of that braid apart and let the silky black texture of her hair flow through his fingertips; to taste that mouth again; faith and saints, he had to get a hold on his feelings. But the woman would never know that just the brush of her fingertips on his when she passed him a biscuit during nooning branded him. She'd never guess that sparks flew every time she looked at him with those gorgeous big aqua-colored eyes. And that was good, because even if she did, it wouldn't change a thing. Tavish had to live with the man who looked back at him when he shaved every morning. He could not live with that man if he did Hank dirty after Hank had been so good to him all those years.

The sun set in a blaze of oranges, pinks and yellows while they finished their supper, everyone talking except Gypsy and Tavish, who kept their thoughts to themselves as they ate in silence.

The hour or two after supper before bedtime was always the longest part of the day for Gypsy. Especially since her arm wasn't healed enough for her to help with many of the chores. She sat at the backside of the wagon and let her gaze fix on the fires across the river. More than 90 women over there, all of them going in the same direction she was. Did any of them ever have doubts about their decisions? She recalled something her grandmother said. Feed your faith and that will drown your doubts. How did Gypsy feed her faith? Faith in what? Her own judgment? Faith that the Almighty wouldn't lead her up to anything he wouldn't lead her through.

She slipped her arm out of the sling and worked on the little cushion of sand Gussie had made. She was supposed to squeeze it 50 times three times a day with her left hand. That, according to Gussie, would keep her from losing the muscle in her arm as it healed. It was getting better each day. Gussie took the stitches out the day before and although it was sore, the scar still red and angry looking, it was healing just fine. She'd been a lucky woman that Gussie was good at doctoring.

She began to count. "Five, where is my faith?" she said aloud and let that question gather wool in her mind for a while.

"Ten. I am miserable and I want out of this decision. Lord please let there be enough women so me and Gussie and Garnet don't have to get married."

Before she could squeeze it five more times she heard an unholy scream from near the river. Connie! More Indians? She was on her feet and running, the sling and the sand-filled miniature sack left behind on the grass. Another scream and a rush of words she thought women weren't ever supposed to even think much less say, filled her ears as she rounded the end of the wagon and saw Connie standing there with her hands on her hips, screaming like a fish wife.

"What in the devil?" Gypsy stopped short when she saw the strange blond-haired woman in Tavish's arms.

"He was kissing her," Connie pointed and shouted. "Kissing her right on the mouth. I saw it. You rat. You worthless Irish gutter rat. You've led me on, making me think you were in love with me and now I find you kissing another woman."

Gypsy stifled a giggle.

"Don't you laugh at me. You know I'm telling the truth. He's been trifling with me ever since he joined the train. He's even asked me to follow him when he leaves," Connie blustered, trying to cover the embarrassment of lies.

"Gypsy," Tavish grinned. "I'd like you to meet my cousin, April. Married and left Chalk Creek last fall. She and her husband put in a horse operation about three miles up the river. When she heard our train was this close, she and her husband came down to see me. Yes, I was kissing her. On the cheek. I'm not so stupid as to think I could kiss her lips. Cecil, would you please leave those horses and come over here?"

"Don't you make excuses," Connie's high-pitched thin voice cut through the night air like a dagger through hot butter. "You're a scoundrel, making love to me one night and then kissing on her the next."

Cecil stepped away from the horses and into the moonlight, slipping his arm around the woman beside Tavish. To Gypsy, he looked like the giant David felled with his sling and stones. Tall, red-haired, and shoulders so broad he could probably uproot a tree with his bare hands.

"See," Tavish laughed, looking right at Gypsy and ignoring Connie. "No one would kiss April with Cecil in sight, and if they did it when he wasn't looking, they'd better be able to run right quick."

"Why are you explaining anything to me? It's your sweetheart, Connie, who's all upset by your actions," Gypsy said.

"Aye, so it is. Connie, please take your lies back to the camp. Go on to bed, lass. I'll not bring it up that you've let your imagination get away from you tonight. Gypsy, please come on closer. We'll sit a spell and visit with my relatives. Good-bye, Connie."

"Tavish, darlin'," Connie giggled, regaining her composure. "You're just trying to make me jealous asking Gypsy to join you. Well, when we are married, I shall make you pay for tonight. Oh, yes, you will pay dearly for it."

"Married?" April raised an eyebrow.

"Not on your dear life, cousin. Especially not to that whining lass. You know me, I'm to be all the children's old bachelor uncle who spoils them," Tavish laughed nervously. "Gypsy, will you join us?"

"No, I'm going to turn in tonight," she said, careful not to say she was going to bed. April looked like a genteel sort and even though she was married, a lady didn't mention a bed in front of gentlemen. At least in polite circles. Wagon train circles were a different matter all together.

"Aye, if you'd be tired, I'll understand, but maybe you could join us just for a bit. What you are doing, going so far from your homes, it's adventurous," April said, her Irish lilt beckoning to Gypsy as much as her outstretched arm. "We only have an hour and must get back. The horses take a lot of time, and day starts early on a horse ranch."

Gypsy couldn't refuse the lady, no more than she could have consented if it had been Connie begging her to stay a spell. She sat and listened while April quizzed Tavish about the kith and kin, learning more and more about the big extended group he called family. She gave him messages to take home to various ones, hugs to bring her mother and father, and send love by the bushels to their grandmother. She laughed when Tavish told her that Gypsy's grandparents' ranch was the place where Paqui hauled the gypsies off to every spring.

"Aye, 'tis a small, small world even though we think it is so big, right, Gypsy?" April turned just in time to catch the look in Gypsy's eye when she looked at Tavish. So that was the way of it. Well, the girl wasn't hard on the eyes and she knew when to keep her mouth shut and listen.

"One more story before you leave," Tavish said.

"Blarney or truth," April said. "I've got a blarney-producing big ox of a husband. If we're going to get a short night's sleep, then I want some truth."

"Oh, my fair cousin, 'tis truth. Every word or the leprechauns can carry me away."

He proceeded to tell them the story of Gypsy getting shot by the Indians and why. High color filled her cheeks as she listened to his version of the tale. It hadn't been nearly that big a deal, or that dangerous. So she'd taken a slug in the arm. It was healing nicely and though she'd carry the scars from it, it wasn't like women folks ran around with their bare arms out for all the public to see. It would be covered all of the time.

"I'm glad you have courage and are not a simpering little pile of whimpering bones and hair," Cecil patted her on the back so hard it jarred a brand new blaze of pain through her arm. "My April steps right up and speaks her mind. Has her own ideas about things. And I'm glad for it. Lightens my load by half."

"Thank you," Gypsy said. *Tell that to your cousin by marriage over there with that grin on his face. He sure doesn't see those as redeeming, glowing qualities in a woman. He called me stupid.*

She said her good-nights before the hour was finished and was tucked snugly in her bedroll when she heard Tavish come back into camp. Connie was wide awake and sat straight up in her bed, her long hair loose, forming a lovely frame for her delicate, young face. Gypsy kept one eye open just a slit to see the fireworks.

"So, that was your cousin. Why didn't you introduce me? Why did you ask Gypsy to stay? I've a mind to tell Hank you've been seeing that half-breed on the sly. We'll see then if you have a job, Mr. High and Mighty Irish," she said barely above a whisper.

"Go to sleep Connie, and remember you signed a paper to be another man's wife too," he said, setting his boots beside his pillow. "And you go tell Hank anything you please, lady. If he believes you, then he doesn't trust me and I don't need the job."

"You are a fool, Tavish. Just like Rafe Pierce was and is. A good thing could jump up and kiss you right on the mouth and you wouldn't know it," she hissed, throwing herself back on the pillow.

*You are probably right,* he thought. *Aye, 'tis a truth, you are right for the first time in your life, Connie. Gypsy did kiss me right on the mouth and I still can not take that which is not mine to take.*

## *Chapter Thirteen*

Fort Bridger was nothing like Gypsy imagined it. She'd thought of a castle-like edifice with a rock wall surrounding it, complete with one of those big cannons in a turret. But Fort Bridger was none of those things in 1860. It was built of logs and daubed with mud, and even in the twilight of the evening with the softening effects of the setting sun, it still looked shabby. Perhaps a dozen lodges of one form or another surrounded the outlying areas of the fort, and she'd overheard Tavish telling Merry that those housed trappers and their Indian wives, when she asked if there would be children at the fort.

Yes, Gypsy thought, there would be children. With skin probably the color of hers and maybe even some with blue eyes. Half-breeds, just like she was, but they wouldn't know, not yet, that the world could be cruel to people who didn't fit into the perfect little molds made up by imperfect people.

They circled their wagons less than a quarter of a mile from the fort, and Hank gave them their orders before they began to make supper. Tomorrow they would have the day to catch up on rest, laundry, mending, cooking, whatever they wanted. They could visit the fort and buy personal supplies if they wanted to do so. Hank would be talking with the brass there and asking if they would like to join the wagon train for a bit of entertainment in the evening hours, tomorrow. If the overseeing officer agreed, then the women could have a social event. They were to remember they were the same as engaged women, promised to be married at the end of this journey, and act with dignity around the soldiers that might be allowed to attend the social. Mormons came to the fort on a regular basis to bring supplies from the outlying areas of Utah Territory, and should they be lucky enough for them to come tomorrow, then Hank promised to purchase eggs and milk, in addition to staples so the ladies could prepare fine foods for their social. He would see to it that all the ladies in the fort were invited.

"And those ladies who live in the lodges?" Gypsy asked. "Will the trappers' wives be invited to sit with us, just as the royalty in that shabby little fort?"

Hank sighed and looked up to heaven. No answers came floating down on the wings of a snow-white dove. Jake Dulan had indeed produced some spitfire daughters in his lifetime. "We will obey the protocol of the area," he said finally. "If it is at all possible we will invite all the women and men to our social. It depends on what the commanding officer says. Sometimes when we stop here and have a layover day, we socialize with the trappers and their wives as well as the fort personnel."

"I see," Gypsy said. "And how many will that be?"

"I think there are a total of twenty-five families in and around the fort. Perhaps twice that many soldiers," Hank said. "So if we can get some eggs and other things you ladies need to work with, you should fix for that many."

"And kids?" Merry asked. "Will there be kids?"

"I don't think there's any right now at the fort, Merry," Hank patted her head. "We'll see what we can do about the lodges and their children."

"Oh, Uncle Hank, beg the officer to let the kids come

and play," Merry said, her eyes glistening amid the freckles dotting her nose.

"One more thing," Hank said just before he left. "The Pony Express uses Fort Bridger for a mail stop. There could possibly be mail for you ladies at the post office. While you are at the fort tomorrow, you should be sure to check for that. And Bobby found out that the Snake Tribe Indians have milk for ten cents a pint and whiskey for two dollars a pint. Would remind you all that the contract you signed said you would not be drinking the whiskey."

A few twitters and giggles sounded throughout the campsite. So far he'd been fortunate in that the women had been true to their contracts where drinking was concerned. But he'd been careful in his interviews to choose women he thought would be good wives. He'd chosen well and they'd been good troupers. There had been a few disagreements but then if there were a hundred men traveling in close quarters there would have been more than just a few catty little spits and fumings.

"Good night ladies," he said. "Enjoy this day because we'll be going through the mountains next, and there will be some long days to get from one camping spot to the next."

An underlying excitement filled the camp that night. Laundry was done early in anticipation of the hopeful social event for the next day. Water barrels were filled; baths taken in the midst of laughing. Merry danced around in her shimmy before bedtime singing a children's song. Annie bustled about trying to get her to calm down for bedtime, assuring her that if she didn't sleep through the night hours, she'd not have the energy to play with the children.

Finally the time came when the women slept and Gypsy stared at the stars. Whatever had made her speak up like that in the camp meeting? Those Indian women who were married to the trappers might not even want to come to some outdoor wagon train social. Their husbands might make them come if they were invited, and the white women of the fort might make them feel like trash under their feet.

"So what are you thinking about so hard that it makes wrinkles on your forehead?" Garnet propped up on one elbow and asked. "You already wishing you'd been nicer to Tavish O'Leary when you had the chance? You know he's going to be gone when we leave Fort Bridger?"

"What?" An acute ache set up in Gypsy's heart.

"Yep," Garnet said. "His job puts him at the front of the wagons from then on. He knows the area even better than Bobby, so they'll trade places. Gives Bobby a rest, Hank told Annie. Tavish leads the wagons through the Wasatch Mountains and that'll take a couple of weeks. Then he'll take us up over something called Little Mountain and down Emigration Canyon. After that we'll go through Echo Canyon and that's where he'll leave us for good. But until then you don't even have to put up with him except at night. By him riding out front, some nights that front wagon will join up with ours when we circle up. Some nights he won't get back in time to do anything but crawl in his bedroll like Bobby does now."

"I see," Gypsy said. Well, that would certainly make it a lot easier on Tavish. He'd said he wouldn't do anything about his feelings for her, and now he could just very well do that. At least he wouldn't have to look at her or be in her presence all day either. Not anymore. And the Irish rat hadn't even had the good grace to tell her himself that after Fort Bridger he would trade places with Bobby. Of course, in the past few days she hadn't so much as given him a glance that he would notice. She'd deliberately shunned him, if she was honest with herself. Why love someone who couldn't return that love, for whatever reasons he deemed important to his dignity and integrity? She flopped over and shut her eyes. Why in the world had she gone and let herself fall in love with a short, cocky little Irishman in the first place?

"Think we might have mail?" Gussie whispered in the silence.

"Yeah, right," Garnet laughed, a deep, resonant laugh, not a high-pitched twitter of a flirting woman. But one of a woman who knew where she was going and what she intended to do when she got there. "I'm just sure all those shirt-tail cousins, aunties and other kith and kin are just waiting in line to send me a note from Arkansas to Fort Bridger," she said. "Lord, Gussie, none of our people even know we signed up on this train. They think we're sitting around in a cabin with our sick father, nursing him back to health. They don't even know there's five of us."

"Yeah, well, I'm just sure there'll be a dozen letters from Tennessee, all addressed to Augusta Dulan," Gussie sighed. "Good night girls. Sounds like we're going to earn that day we get tomorrow. The next couple of weeks sound like a real trial."

"Sure does," Gypsy whispered. The trial wasn't in the next two weeks though. It would be in the time after that, when Tavish would be gone for good. When one part of her would be thankful not to have that Irish grin staring at her every moment of the day; when the other part would be aching just to look at the sight of him, with that short-man swagger and cockiness begging for an argument. Trials were nothing more than the opposition between two forces, and the trial had already begun in Gypsy's heart.

The next morning she and her sisters were the first ones out of the circle and at the fort. Needing nothing but the familiarity of something that even faintly resembled a town, they strolled into the general store and looked at everything there. The storekeeper's wife was friendly enough, promising that she would indeed come down to the camp that evening and would bring her famous sweet potato pie for the refreshment table. She also told them that the new commanding officer had a good relationship with the traders and their Indian wives and she was sure those women would probably join the wagon train social.

By mid-afternoon the whole area was in a hubbub of excitement. The 15 women who lived in the confines of the fort baked cakes and pies, fussed and fumed over their hair and attire and looked forward to an evening with the women who'd been strong enough to endure months on a wagon train; who had the absolute nerve to undertake something like that. The 12 Indian women who were trappers' wives made food, made their children take baths even though it wasn't the traditional night for that activity, and looked forward to sitting with the women who were strong enough to walk across the world to find a home and husband. That they respected.

The inside of the circle became a plantation home parlor. Fires were laid back away from the center so there would be room for dancing. Makeshift tables were set up, with much discussion of how to place them for easiest access. They wished for fruit to squeeze to make real punch, but decided that tea would have to do, and that would be served from a watering pail. Garnet stood back and looked long and hard at the tables, filling up by late afternoon with cakes and pies made with milk and eggs bought from the Snake Tribe women.

"Okay, ladies, listen up," Garnet said loudly. "We'd all love to have a crystal punch bowl filled up with pretty fruit punch and ice floating in it. But we can't make silk purses out of sows' ears. What we have is a water pail with a rope bail and we're lucky to have tea to brew and a little sugar to sweeten it with. So what I suggest is that since this can't really be a fancy dress ball, that we work with what we have and stop bemoaning what we ain't got. There's enough wild flowers out there in the fields to decorate this place up, and we got water and quart jars to put them in. Let's make this a party with what we got, like we did when that young couple got married. They thought our wedding feast was wonderful."

"But these are ladies from the fort," Connie laid her hand on her forehead. "They are used to finer things."

"Look at that fort. They're probably just glad to see some other women to talk to," Annie said. "Connie, why don't you and Bertie be in charge of the wild flower decorations. I'm sure you can arrange flowers beautifully."

"Of course I can," Connie sniffed. At least Annie realized that Connie and Bertie could take care of the most important part of the social better than anyone else. "Come on Bertie, grab that bushel basket and let's go pick flowers."

"Thank you!" Gussie whispered. "Any more of her airs and we'd all be ready to have a lynching before the party."

"Blessed are the peacemakers," Gypsy uttered with a laugh.

"Hey, Gussie," Merry yelled, coming across the open field in a dead run and waving. "Hey, Gussie there's two letters for you and one for Annie."

Gussie stopped in her tracks, a chill working its way up through the sweat running down her backbone. Letters. How did anyone know to write her at Fort Bridger? That and a thousand other questions blasted through her mind like a tornado in search of answers.

"Oh, it's from my brother," Annie grabbed the letter from Merry and held it to her chest. "I told him we'd be going past Fort Kearny and then Fort Bridger and he could write me a letter at one of those places. That's why I sent Merry to check. I was afraid to go for fear it wouldn't be there and I'd just be disappointed."

Gussie reached out with shaking hands to accept the two envelopes from Merry. Garnet and Gypsy gathered close to her. Bad news. It had to be bad news from her family in Tennessee. They would have somehow found out from the people at the hotel in St. Joseph that Gussie had gone with the wagon train and sent a letter to the Pony Express station in Fort Bridger.

Gussie held them for the longest time, clutched to her chest, afraid to even look at them. Without looking, she knew in the depths of her heart, they were from an officer at Fort Laramie, telling her and her sisters that Velvet had died.

"Well?" Gypsy raised a dark eyebrow.

Gussie handed both of the letters to Gypsy. "You read them. Come and sit beside me and Garnet and you read them. I can't even look at them, Gypsy. You're the strong one. You'll have to read them."

"I'm not a whit stronger than either of you," she took the letters from Gussie's hand. "But I'll read them. Let's find a place outside the circle."

Garnet grabbed a pieced quilt and smoothed it out on the grass a few yards from the circle. She sat down beside Gussie and Gypsy joined them. Which one to read first? She looked at the return addresses. One from Willow Dulan Pierce in Nebraska. The other from Velvet Dulan Baxter in Fort Laramie, Wyoming. Gypsy smiled and opened Velvet's letter first. It would assure Gussie that Velvet was well enough to write a letter anyway. She began to read:

My dearest sisters,

I have survived the awful fever, thanks to Dr. Hoyt Baxter, who is now my husband as of two days ago. We have a lovely little ranch just outside of Fort Laramie, and although Hoyt is going back to the Fort to be their physician, we don't know if we will stay here past this winter or not. With the coming war, we may decide to go back to Louisiana where he is from. I told him that I don't care where we live. Anywhere he is will be my promised land. Remember what the man said to Willow about there wasn't no promised land? Well there is, my sisters. Only, it's not a place or a destination. It's a journey with the person you love, and I've found mine. Be happy for me. And let's plan a reunion in a few years. I wish we weren't so scattered but I'm not so sure the world could have taken five Dulans in one spot anyway. I love you all.

Am also sending a letter to Willow to let her know about my good fortune and wonderful new life.
Signed, Velvet Jane Dulan Baxter.

"Well, I'll be hanged," Gussie shook her head. "If that don't beat all. Velvet married to the very doctor who saved her. Now that would be a story worth hearing at our reunion, wouldn't it?"

"And when is this reunion going to be?" Garnet asked.

"How about in ten years?" Gypsy said. "Right back at St. Joseph, Missouri, and we'll go visit Jake's grave and put flowers on it."

"Sounds like a wonderful plan to me," Garnet said. "We ought to leave a couple of letters here for the Pony Express to take to Willow and Velvet. Let them know we're still alive and that we made it this far."

"The other letter is from Willow," Gypsy said, carefully opening the envelope. She read a long, newsy letter to them about the ranch where she and Rafe lived; her darling sister-in-law and the nieces and nephews that had stolen her heart, the horses and the people in the town, the church and how she'd found her own bit of the promised land right there in the middle of Nebraska. She, too, mentioned a reunion amongst the five of them sometime in the future when they were all settled and one could be arranged.

Gypsy read both letters again and then handed them back to Gussie. "Put them in a safe place and we'll read them again later. When we're tired and think we can't go on another foot, they'll give us hope."

Gussie nodded. Garnet picked up the quilt, wiped away a tear and hoped neither of her sisters noticed. It would take more than those two letters to keep her going much longer. Especially if Gypsy ever woke up and admitted the attraction she held for Tavish O'Leary. That two of her sisters were already settled and happy in their own chunk of the promised land didn't mean that there was a portion of that bright land for Garnet Diana. No sir, no guarantees at all.

The three of them traipsed back to the hustle and bustle of the party preparations, each mulling over the letters they'd received; each wondering where life would lead them.

"Well, look here, if it ain't the Dulan girls," Tavish said from the middle of the grassy parlor with the promise of a starlit ceiling when the sun had fully set.

Gypsy hadn't even thought of roses and yet, there he was. Had he started appearing even when she wasn't trying to conjure up a vision of the future? Evidently he had because there he stood, just bigger than life itself. Dark eyes, as misplaced in all that Irish background, as her own blue eyes were in her Mexican skin; an impish grin that promised quick wit even if she was in the mood for a good fight; and a cocky stance just begging for her to sling her arms around his neck and bring his lips down for a passionate kiss.

High color filled her cheeks at the idea of that. "Hello," she mumbled as she brushed past him, not even remotely amazed at the sparkling aura flashing when their arms even touched.

"And a fine day to you, Gypsy," he said. "Is your program book all filled for the night or will you save me a dance?"

"It's filling fast," she had to smile. "But since you have asked so nicely, I shall pencil you in for the last dance."

"Oh, the last one. I'm honored," Tavish bowed deeply from the waist. "Aye, 'tis the fellow who dances the last dance with an Irish lass who has her heart in his pocket."

"Who says?" Gypsy asked, her eyes wide with mortification. Lord, she'd had no idea that was a tradition thing with the Irish.

"Well, the leprechauns, the fairies and Tavish O'Leary, who just made that up on the spot," he chuckled.

She slapped his shoulder with her good arm and pranced

away, not knowing whether to let the anger or the laughter have first place. Gussie and Garnet were both succumbing to the giggles when she reached their sides, so the anger had to take a back seat as they locked arms and paraded through the open air ballroom. Everything was in order. In a few minutes the guests would arrive. Merry danced around like she had a whole bed of red ants in her pantaloons. The rest of the women waited . . . or fussed with the tables.

The trappers arrived first, bringing their wives and more importantly their children. Merry made friends rapidly and Gypsy stood in the shadows watching her and the children exchange stories. She could tell them about places they'd never see; they could tell her about their settled lives. It took all of half an hour and then the whole bunch of them were off in the fields chasing fireflies, the sound of their laughter piercing through the twilight of the evening. None of them cared that she had red hair and blue eyes with a fair sprinkling of freckles across her nose. She didn't care that their skin was the same color as Gypsy's, that most of them had Indian dark eyes and every shade of brown hair in the world.

A fiddler played a lively tune off to one side of the circle where women sat on pallets thrown on the grass and visited amongst themselves. Women from the fort who wanted information about where the wagon train ladies had been and what they'd seen. Women from the lodges, who like the rest of them had opinions and ideas about everything from raising children to taming wild men for husbands. Gypsy tapped her foot in time to the music and finally, sure that Merry was fitting in with the children, joined a group of women on a quilt.

"Well, Connie hasn't set out a single dance," Gussie laughed.

"Did you expect her to?" Gypsy spread the skirt of her best calico dress around herself as she sat down gracefully, just glad that she could do so now without help. Her arm still pained her but it was better enough that she could leave off the sling for tonight anyway.

"Every group has a Connie," the commanding officer's wife said with a sly smile. "Ours is Myrtle, over there in the pink dress with white lace. She's the poor martyr no one appreciates, who's the first to spread any tidbit of malicious gossip, who flirts with the new young soldiers even though she has a husband. The grass is always greener on the other side, you know."

"And ours is right over there," a tall, beautiful dark-haired Indian woman said. "The one with the red calico dress. She's the one who is always at my front door when her own husband is off on the trapping lines. Who wants to flirt around my husband. Her name is Rosie. Of the Snake Indians like the rest of us, I'm sorry to admit. Are you part Indian?"

Gypsy slowly shook her head. "No, half Mexican," she said.

"I thought you might be Indian with that lovely skin. I hope my daughters have skin like that when they are grown, and what I wouldn't have given for one of them to have your strange blue eyes. But me and Elijah both have brown eyes so that would be too much I guess."

"Thank you," Gypsy said honestly. Suddenly she saw another world before her in the midst of fiddle music joined in with a guitar and a banjo. One where Indians, whites and every other nationality lived together in peace. It might be a long time coming, but it would arrive. She might never see it, but that didn't matter either. And right then she figured if that kind of world were ever to materialize it had to begin with people like her . . . half-breeds. She shook the chip from her shoulder as deftly as if it had really been a heavy load. Time to let go of all that, she decided. Life would be what she, Maria Marguerite Gypsy Rose Dulan, made it. She was a strong woman who knew her mind, and she wasn't sitting back on a stump letting life pass her by because she was a blue-eyed Mexican.

"Mercy, what are you thinking about again that brings wrinkles to your face? Tavish O'Leary again?" Garnet sat down with less grace than she'd have liked.

"Not this time. I was thinking about life. Seems human nature is the same whether it's amongst women on a wagon train, women over there in the fort or those in the lodges."

"Sure enough is," the Indian woman said. "We get born with human nature no matter where we live."

"Well, let's not dwell on such serious thoughts this night. Music and dancing. I miss them both. How 'bout you, Gussie?" Garnet changed the subject.

"You bet I do. I danced in saloons before I came to St. Joseph, Missouri," Gussie explained to the women on the quilt.

"Did you really?" The commander's wife asked, her blue eyes twinkling in a bed of wrinkles. "Tell me about it. I do love an independent woman. Do you ever think we'll have the vote?"

"Aye, someday," Tavish stepped out of the darkness behind the wagon. "And I bet the women in this group will be first in line. Now, Miss Dulan, you have promised me a dance." He held out his hand.

"I did at that, but I don't believe this is the last dance. The night is still young," Gypsy looked up at him from beneath heavy lashes and dark eyebrows.

His heart stood still, frozen in the moment. "Aye, you are right. But this poor beggar Irishman is asking for a little waltz to hold him until the last dance."

"Oh, okay," Gypsy said, ignoring the looks from Garnet and the prodding on her backbone from Gussie that no one could see though she could feel it well enough.

She melted into his arms as if she'd waited her whole life to be there. He held her close enough to feel the beat of her heart in unison with his and slowly began a waltz that was so graceful others stepped back to watch them. But Tavish and Gypsy scarcely saw them. They danced in a private world, a ballroom with a full moon, a ceiling full of twinkling stars and two hearts blending as one, keeping time with the slow beat of the music.

*Te quiero,* she thought, but didn't say a word because to do so would only bring more pain and heartache.

"Don't they look lovely together? They are in love, aren't they? Look at the way they look at each other," the Indian lady said.

"Yes, they do," Garnet said. "And yes they are in love but they're both stubborn and I'm afraid they'll never admit what is in their hearts."

"Then tonight I shall make a . . ." the Indian lady laughed. "I won't tell you. I shall just help them along."

"I'm not so sure I want you to do that," Gussie said. "I want her to be with me and Garnet in California, not running off to some horse ranch in Utah Territory."

"The thing I'll do will only work on hearts that beat as one," the Indian lady laughed. "Now shall we go and cut some of those lovely cakes and let these soldier boys and trappers have a little feast? They have all been very good to dance and play for our evening when they are all dying to talk war. We can serve refreshments and let them have their men talk, tell their stories."

"Thank you for the dance," Gypsy curtsied when Tavish brought her back to the quilt. "It was lovely and you dance wonderfully well."

"Aye, 'tis the Irish. Ma said that my good looks would take me far in life but charm would get me anything I wanted," he said with that familiar glitter in his eyes.

"Your ma gave you good advice," Gypsy said in a moment of peace with him. "But charm only works on women like Connie. Not a bull-headed one like me."

"We'll see," Tavish said. "I see we are about to cut into all that wonderful food. Don't sit down. Let me lead your through the line and we'll enjoy some of Annie's chocolate cake together as we watch the children."

For some crazy reason, she didn't argue with him.

# *Chapter Fourteen*

Nothing had prepared the women for the journey through the Wasatch Mountains. It was as if they left civilization when they hitched up their wagons and drove away from Fort Bridger that next morning. Bobby rode at the back of the train, just like Garnet had said. Gypsy drove through ruts that first day that hardly seemed wide enough to accommodate the wagon. Steep inclines rose straight up to the clouds on both sides of the pitted, rough road choked with willows and brush.

Merry rode beside her, chattering about the children she'd played with. Gypsy listened with half an ear, nodding occasionally so Merry would think she had her full attention. Gussie, Garnet and Annie walked along beside the wagon, much closer than usual since the trail was so narrow. Gypsy wondered if there would be a place big enough to circle the wagons by the end of the day.

The mountains were lovely, to be sure. But somehow they stifled her. She compared them with the situation between her and Tavish. Lovely, but enough to smother the breath from her lungs. There was a narrow path through their feelings, but there were insurmountable problems on both sides of the path. On one side was the mountainous piece of paper she'd signed saying she would marry a man at the end of the trip. On that same side was his dignity and integrity in not trespassing on another man's territory. The other side of the path was the mountain called Gypsy and her own determination.

She looked up at the sun's rays filtering down through the clouds. As if saying, there's a silver lining inside the dark clouds. See the lovely gossamer rays. That's the promise of something wonderful.

"Hmmph," she snorted.

"What was that all about?" Garnet asked.

"Did Uncle Tavish kiss you last night?" Merry asked.

"You think we'll get there with a woman to spare?" Annie asked.

"Not if I shoot Connie," Gussie laughed. "What do you think, Gypsy, shall I shoot her or not?"

"Mercy me, I'm glad I didn't utter a whole sentence if one little snort can bring on that many questions." Gypsy had to laugh. "To answer you, Garnet, I was thinking of Tavish and how all the problems around us are as big as these mountains. Merry, no, Tavish didn't kiss me last night. He knows I'm already the same as engaged to another man and he's a proper man. Annie, why are you asking about an extra woman? You got second thoughts? And Gussie, darlin', if you'll shoot Connie, I'll provide the bullet, and take the blame."

"Why?" Merry asked innocently.

"Why what?" Gypsy kept her eyes on the wagon in front of them.

"Why didn't he kiss you? I know you said you'd marry up with a man when we get to California, but that don't mean he can't kiss you or that you can't fall in love with him, does it?"

"It's got something to do with a man's feelings about himself. If he's got integrity then he doesn't take another man's woman."

"Then tell him to give the integrity to Uncle Hank," Merry said. "Uncle Hank can throw it away like all that stuff we see on the side of the road. Is integrity a piece of paper or is it something a man puts in his saddlebags?"

Amidst the laughter, Gypsy wondered why everything between them had become such a big mountain anyway. If he really loved her he would offer to buy the contract from Hank. Maybe love came in degrees with a man like Tavish. Was Gypsy worth the price of a couple or three good mares?

That settled into her heart like a dose of bitter herbs. By nooning she was still quiet, contemplating whether she'd even want a permanent commitment from Tavish if he wouldn't even pay the price of a few horses for her contract. The women spread out the leftovers from the feast the night before, and they wandered up and down the stretched-out wagon train, sampling cakes, pies, cold buffalo steaks and sliced venison roast.

"Well, hello, Gypsy, ain't you a fair sight for an Irishman's eyes this morning," Tavish said as he reached for a slab of Annie's chocolate cake.

"I wouldn't know," she smarted off at him, flaunting her skirt tail as she turned and marched off to the side of the wagons as far as she could without getting tangled in the underbrush of willow thicket.

"What's the matter with her?" Tavish asked Annie.

"I wouldn't know."

"Last night she was as sweet as honey on a fresh slice of bread. Today she's all vinegar and sour pickles," Tavish said.

Women! He'd never understand them. He went back to the front of the wagons, mounted his horse and waited for Hank to give the signal. Faith and saints, he didn't need a woman with so many moods he couldn't count them. He wanted a woman who'd be the same every day; who'd wait for him on the porch at the end of the day, with sweet smells of baking coming through the door; who'd snuggle up beside him in the bed at night and ask him about his day.

*Sure you do,* his conscience rebuked. *That would be all fine and good for a week. Two at the most. But at the end of that, you'd be crazy. You need a woman to keep you on your toes. One who can work beside you all day with the horses, throw a supper together in record time, not be afraid to jump in the creek with you for a bath, and then fall into the bed with you. You want a woman who speaks her mind even if she doesn't agree with you. One just exactly like your mother, Tavish O'Leary. A good hard-working, hard-hitting woman who'll raise your kids and keep you on your toes all your life. Who'll keep the sparkle in your eyes the way it is in your Da's eyes.*

"Aye, maybe so," he mumbled under his breath, "but her name ain't Gypsy Dulan."

To Gypsy's surprise there was a small meadow seemingly cut to just the right size for their wagons to circle up in that evening. The oxen and horses had little room outside the circle but what there was provided rich, green grass and the nearby river gave them plenty of water. Gypsy had read about an oasis but she thought they were little places with strange palm trees in the middle of deserts. That an oasis could be right smack in the middle of a mountain range was truly a miracle. She pulled off her gloves, tossed them into the back of the wagon and flexed her arm. It had been the first day the other ladies had allowed her to drive and the job had taxed her strength.

"Hard day?" Bobby asked, making the rounds, checking on all the women before he joined the men at a makeshift camp right at the base of a tall, brush-covered mountain.

"I'll survive," Gypsy said.

"Dulans usually do," Bobby laughed and went on to the next train.

Supper was more leftover feast fare. Merry didn't mind one bit as she ran from wagon to wagon, sampling a cookie here, a sliver of pie there. Gypsy kept expecting to look up any moment and see Tavish swaggering around but he stayed in the men's camp all evening. Well, that was fine with her, she kept telling her crazy fluttering heart. She didn't need him anyway, and if he'd stay out of her sight, then he'd pretty soon be out of her mind.

Just before she pulled the covers up to her neck for the night, she reread the two letters aloud. Once she was settled in for the night, she let the ambiance of what they'd written sink into her heart and she was jealous. Not the ugly kind of jealousy that eats away at a woman's soul, leaving her bitter. But the kind that looks on from a distance and wants that same thing for their own. Velvet, married to the very doctor who'd brought her back from death's door. And such love written between the lines in the letter. And Willow. Well, no one ever doubted that Willow and Rafe would be happy. That was written in the stars.

Gypsy rolled over and peeped out at a slice of sky high up between the mountains. Mountains behind them, ahead of them, on each side, with only a ribbon of stars straight up ahead of her. Secrets, Paqui had said, would be opened to her if she studied the stars. One thing for sure, if there were secrets there they were in the stars the mountains were covering up. And even though her sisters had found their promised land, she doubted if there was a chunk of promised land out there anywhere with her name on it. She'd just have to be content knowing that two of the five Dulan girls had found theirs, and go on with living. She had very little choice anyway.

Three days later, the novelty of Echo Canyon had worn off. Merry had sent her voice out in every way possible just to hear it return to her. The wagons, rolling along on their iron wheels, sounded like hammers resounding in the canyon. Noise redoubled everywhere and all Gypsy wanted was a few minutes of peace and quiet. Would they never get out of this 25-mile canyon?

On the fourth day, the noise factor reduced by half but Gypsy's edginess didn't. Tavish kept his distance, and since Independence Rock when he'd joined the wagons, she hadn't gone four whole days without at least one major altercation with him. She wished he'd come around just so she could give him a healthy portion of her mind. Then in the same second, she hoped he just rode away to his precious Chalk Creek town one morning and she never heard from him again. If he was truly gone then she'd have to forget him. She'd have absolutely no choice.

By the end of the 10th day, they were following a trail so narrow the women had to ride in the wagons, and they planned to travel only five miles that day. A high mountain range extended halfway to heaven itself on their right, and the river snaked along on their left. There was no walking space on either side for the women. Merry was restless, cooped up in the back of the narrow confines of an overstuffed wagon all day. Gussie kept her busy on her patchwork quilt but even that was a chore after nooning when they even had to eat their lunch inside the wagon. Garnet entertained them by singing and Gypsy told stories of the ranch in Texas. By the end of the day when Tavish had found their next little oasis in a small valley, they were all ready to climb out of the wagon and never complain about walking again.

"What is that?" Merry pointed to a group of strange rocks.

"Witches Rocks," Tavish said so close to Gypsy's neck she could feel the warmth of his breath on her tender skin.

"Oh, Uncle Tavish," Merry ran and jumped into his arms. "Where have you been? I thought you'd run off without telling me good-bye."

"Not for three or four more days, darlin'," he said. "I ought to tell you good-bye now, so if I don't see you again, it will be done."

"Okay," Merry said seriously. "We'll say them now and then if you do see me again we won't talk about it. I don't like good-byes, Uncle Tavish. I had to tell Velvet good-bye and I was afraid she would die. And I had to tell Willow good-bye and Uncle Rafe. So good-bye, Uncle

Tavish," she giggled and ran off toward the center of the circle where Annie and other women were busy preparing two cauldrons of stew.

"Good-bye my child," he whispered.

"Ain't easy, is it?" Gypsy asked.

"Never is, especially if a person is very fond of another," he said, turned heel and disappeared so fast she wondered if he'd really been there.

Ah, but the heat down deep in her body said he'd left behind an aura that hung on to her heart like a bulldog with a big meaty ham bone. She sighed and went about her chores. So much for the out-of-sight-out-of-mind theory. It didn't work one bit better than that mumbo-jumbo about the scent of roses giving a person the power to see into the future.

The further the sun set, the worse the restlessness in her heart became. Finally, she told the other women she was going for a walk and set out in the direction of those weird rocks. She bypassed Hank and Bobby on the way, told them she was out for a bit of quiet and Hank advised her to be careful. An hour later, the light from the sun had completely blinked out and the moon and stars lit up the Witches Rocks, standing like an eerie silent sentinel. She walked on, not caring that it would take her equally as long to get back to the wagons. They drew her toward them as surely as if they were really witches; really waiting to tell her something profound.

In an hour she sat down on the bare ground and stared at them, still no closer or further than they'd been when she started. It would take hours and hours to stand so close she could touch those rocks. And then what? They were simply tall, jutting rocks, left over from years and years of wind, rain, ice and storms. Even if she could touch them they'd be no more than rocks. They didn't have a soul. No heart. No breath in them. They couldn't tell her anything.

The first growl that broke the silence made her jump. But she convinced herself it was just a play on her imagination. Witches Rocks? Why hadn't they called them Mormon Rocks or Angel Rocks? If they had she'd have seen someone like Malachi Brubaker, a Mormon who'd tried to get Willow to marry him, standing before her. Or if they'd been Angel Rocks, no doubt, her mind would have conjured up a vision of a lovely heavenly figure with big fluffy white wings and a halo.

The second growl got her attention and she fingered the dagger she carried. The low, sinister growl was no figment of anyone's imagination. It sounded like a bear or a coyote. She sat still, moving only her eyes in a sweeping scan around the area. When she reached the small outcropping of brush just to her left she felt, rather than saw the presence. Every hair on her arms stood at attention. In spite of the cool night breeze, fear became sweat and trickled down her backbone.

She pulled the knife from the sheath and held it in readiness. A bear would tear her to shreds; a coyote, she might take out before he tore her up too badly. The third deep throated snarl was closer, and yellow eyes, illuminated by the light of the moon, peeped out at her from the brush. A big cat or a coyote. Either one might run away if she made some noise.

She opened her mouth to scream just as the mountain lion cleared the brush with one jump and opened it's big mouth to scream at her for invading his territory. She drew the knife up and was on her feet in an instant. The lion bounded again, a shot rang out in the dark and the big cat fell from the sky like a shooting star, to lay at her feet. The bullet had caught it right between the eyes and it looked strangely beautiful in death, lying there so peaceful and serene.

Gypsy began to tremble in spite of the warmth of the animal stretched out against her toes. It's claws were ferocious looking; it's mouth big enough to quite literally bite off her arm. She jumped and drew back the knife when someone touched her, fear still rushing through her veins with such speed it made the top of her head ache.

"Hey, hey, it's me," Tavish said, grabbing her arm and holding it at bay.

"What are you doing out here?" She buried her head in his chest and let the tremors run their course. "Lord, Tavish, I thought I'd seen my last star-lit night."

"I know," he held her tight, soothing her with the Irish lilt of his voice and the racing beat of his own heart. "If I hadn't killed him with that shot, he would have mauled you even though I hit him. I was scared to death."

"You, an Irishman full of blarney, was scared?" She pulled back to look at him. Sure enough, his face was chalky white. The witches rocks just over his left shoulder were the same ghostly color.

"I expect we're even now," she said. "I saved you from the snake and you've taken care of this mountain lion in addition to the mean man who tried to kidnap me. Matter of fact, I guess I'm owing you one now."

"Could be, but that was a big snake and I hate snakes," he said. "Want to take it back to camp and skin it out for a rug?"

"I don't want to touch it. Let the buzzards have it for breakfast," she said with another shiver.

"It's dead," he said, tilting her chin back. "Of course, we'll leave it. Gypsy?"

"Tavish?"

Lip met lip in a kiss that practically made the Witches Rocks sway in the gentle moonlight breeze. A song went out from two hearts that hummed in the glitter of the stars. Two souls mourned for what could not be.

## *Chapter Fifteen*

"Where you been?" Garnet whispered into the stillness of the night when Gypsy quietly removed her boots and stretched out in her bedroll one of her sisters had been kind enough to prepare for her.

"Out killing mountain lions," Gypsy whispered back.

"Sure you have. Was his name Tavish O'Leary?"

"No, I didn't ask his name. Good night, Garnet. Thanks for waiting up for me."

"I was going to give you another five minutes then I was coming after you, girl. Sleep well. Tomorrow you drive. Only a couple of more days and we're out of this and back into some flat land."

"Good," Gypsy said and rolled over, shut her eyes and went to sleep. Only to dream of battling mountain lions, snakes, foul-smelling men and Indians. All the while, Tavish fought beside her and when they'd slain the last of their foes, he drew her into his arms for a lingering kiss. She awoke, her heart speeding, and she didn't know whether it was because of the kiss in her dream, the one in reality, or the battles they'd fought and won together.

That day they followed the snaking Weber River all day long and she didn't see Tavish at all. The next day they spent the day double-teaming the wagons and literally pushing and pulling them up the side of Little Mountain. When each wagon reached the summit, they unlocked the brake and let them slide down the other side into Emigration Canyon. By the end of the day, the women were hot, snarly and sweaty and the river never looked so good. Not even in the chill of the evening did they complain about wanting hot water and a real tub to wash away the sweat and toil of that day.

Gypsy and her sisters, along with everyone else on the train, checked their wagons for damage. Satisfied that the wheels would still roll the next day, that the wooden parts of the wagon were intact, the dingy gray sheet that had been so pretty and white in the beginning mended where a tree limb ripped it, they finally crawled into their beds, sighed and gave thanks that every day wasn't like the ones they'd just experienced.

Hank gave them a pep talk the next morning, telling them they'd done very well. That he'd taken many trains through the mountains and down through the canyon with plenty of men folks, and none of them had endured the whole journey any better than the women had done. That brought on a round of applause and a high sniff from Connie who no doubt thought she should have individual praise. Now they'd travel a few days, then there would be a 65 mile desert to cross. Hank said they'd make it in five days and the water in the barrels would have to suffice. They'd stop in a community called Chinatown for a day and then at Frenchman's Ford for a last oasis on the Humboldt River before they slid on into California, hoping to be through the Rockies and to Bryte in about 10 more weeks.

"Questions?" he asked.

"Yes," Merry raised her hand like a dutiful student in a school room.

"No, I don't know if there are any kids you can get acquainted with in Chinatown, darlin', but if there's one within ten miles, I bet he or she will just happen to be in town on the day we go through."

"Well, Uncle Hank, that's sure good to know, but what I wanted to know is who is the fellow standing right behind you? He just walked up there and I don't think we know him."

Hank adjusted the glasses perched on the end of his nose and turned slowly, a smile etching its way across his face. "This is Homer. He's our new helper."

"Hello," the man nodded seriously. His gray hair, cut short, looked out of place on top of a face covered with wrinkles so deep and numerous they looked like lines on a map. "I'm Homer Haskell. Here to take Tavish O'Leary's place. I'll be going on the rest of the journey with you ladies. Understand you've done right well up to here. Well, the men at the end are eager for you to get there. That's where I've come from. My nephew, Jack Haskell, is one of the men waiting for a new bride. It's a tough ride from here on in, but you've had a tough journey so you can make it."

"Are you waiting for a bride?" Merry asked.

"No, ma'am," he tipped his hat toward the little girl. "But if I was, I'd sure hope it would be you."

"Oh, I'm too little to think about husbands," Merry said. "Besides, you'll be dead by the time I'm old enough to marry."

Homer threw back his head and roared, a deep laughter that filled the whole camp, causing twitters behind palms and Annie to whisper words of correction to Merry. "No," Homer threw up his hand when Merry started to apologize with a reddened face, "don't say you are sorry, my child. That was the funniest thing I've heard in a month. It takes a lot to make old Homer laugh. I think me and you are going to get along fine, and I know just the man in Bryte who needs a daughter just like you."

"Is Uncle Tavish gone then?" Merry asked.

"Left out about thirty minutes ago. When I rode up to

the camp, he was mounting his horse. Said since I was there he'd just ride on out to his ranch. He's Irish you know and they tend to hate good-byes. We've worked trains back to back for a long time now. He most usually just tells me to tell everyone to have a safe and happy journey."

Tavish was gone.

Gone.

Finally.

Gypsy's heart fell down into her boots and lay there in a broken, shattered heap of pure pain. It's what she'd wanted from the first time he'd put his nasty old boot on her leg and shoved her, calling her a squaw. So, if it was truly what she wanted so badly, then why did it hurt so much?

Glad she didn't have to drive that day, she lingered behind the other women, listening to them make out a dozen questions each to ask Homer when the day was finished. Gypsy couldn't think of a single thing she wanted to know about Bryte, California. Not one thing. She didn't want to know about the men there, the stores, the church. Nothing. She just wanted the ache in her heart to subside and the void in her soul to fill back up with something even if it was anger. Anything would be better than the hole full of nothing without Tavish O'Leary.

She barely nibbled at the edges of her food during the nooning, knowing that the gnawing nerves in her stomach would rebel if she swallowed. Besides, the lump in her throat made it difficult to get anything down anyway. She tried to force her thoughts away from Tavish all afternoon as she walked beside the wagon. She didn't love him, and if she did, she'd get over it. She'd live on memories of that one last kiss with the Witches Rocks in the distance over his shoulder. She'd forget the kiss and never think of it again. She'd never marry another man because she was in love with Tavish. She'd marry the man whose name got drawn with hers out of the hat, and never think of him again.

By evening, they made camp at a deep Y in the road. The left fork led into Utah, toward Tavish and Chalk Creek. The other fork, the one they'd take tomorrow, would lead them through the desert land toward a little place called Chinatown and then one named Frenchman's Ford, and then they'd go south from there into California. Through more desert and finally to the town where husbands waited for their brides.

"You're sure quiet tonight," Gussie said. "You know, I expected you to go with him. Right up to the end, I expected it, but you didn't."

"Want to know why?" Gypsy asked. "Well, I'll tell you why, Gussie. It's because he didn't ask me. I don't know what I would have answered. Lord, all we did was rub each other wrong. I can't imagine a life like that, where all we do is argue. But I can't imagine a life with some humdrum man, either. Not even one who thinks I'm the best thing in the world. He didn't ask me because he's got all this Irish integrity that says I'm already asked for and given my vow to marry another man. At least that's the curtain he's hiding behind. I think it's because he knows if he has to buy my contract from Hank, he won't have the money for the horses to finish his herd."

"Do you really think that?" Gussie asked. "Because if you do, then you don't need him anyway."

"Truth? I don't know what I think, if I'm honest. I say that because I need something to be mad about, and I want to be mad for the rest of the trip," Gypsy said with a wave of her hand. "So let's not think about Tavish right now. What did you ply out of Homer?"

"That Bryte is a booming little town. Got a church with a preacher man who's got his name in the hat for a wife too. I hope Connie gets him. Maybe he can make her stay on her knees every night and she'll get all that haughtiness out of her. That there's a school which will suit Merry to a tee since there will be kids there, but I've got a feeling

Merry won't be staying in Bryte," Gussie whispered conspiratorially.

"Oh?" Gypsy raised a dark eyebrow.

"Annie is in love with Hank. If we get there with too many women I bet she proposes to him."

"Women don't do that," Gypsy said.

"Some do. If it's necessary," Gussie said. "Sometimes a man just don't have the nerve to stand up and say what is in his heart. Rafe came back for Willow, remember? But by golly, if he hadn't, she would have marched right up to his door and asked him to marry her. I don't have a doubt about it, and she would've done it in her overalls and her old weathered hat too. I can't wait to hear the whole story about Velvet. What do you bet, she sure didn't stammer around when she figured out what she wanted?"

"No, I reckon she found that old Dulan backbone when she needed it," Garnet said, joining in the conversation.

"What'd you find out about Bryte?" Gussie asked Garnet.

"Just that there's a saloon and there's a piano in it. So I'm planning on playing that piano. You two can come visit me and tell me all about your little home life. There's going to be enough women that I'm not marrying anyone."

"Oh, Garnet, you'll change your mind," Gussie said.

"Nope, I will not."

Gypsy listened to Gussie's and Garnet's easy banter about Bryte. What an ingenious idea Hank had in bringing Homer in on the trip at this point. The women were bone weary from the journey, especially the last two weeks since they'd left Fort Bridger. Now they could ask questions and Homer could entertain them about the residents of Bryte the rest of the way. By the time they'd crossed those deserts and walked into that town, they'd know names and have an idea of what kind of town they'd be living in. Yes, sir, Hank was a genius.

One idea after another flitted through Gypsy's mind as she tried to sleep that night. Nothing made a bit of sense.

Hate for Tavish had turned to love. His ghost rose from the ashes where she thought she'd burned his memory that morning when she'd found he was gone. She smiled at the sight of him shivering and shaking his arm where the snake had touched him; suppressed a giggle at him lying on the ground underneath her with a knife blade at his throat. What was it he called that sharp two-edged dagger she kept company with? Oh, yes, a *bodkin*. Well, he'd learned a healthy respect for that *bodkin* when she'd slung it at the snake. Then there was the wild fury in his eyes when he threatened to shoot that giant of a man who abducted her, and the way his heart raced when he'd killed the mountain lion about to have her for a late night snack.

She pushed her way out from under the wagon and propped her back against the wagon wheel, staring without blinking at the stars. Paqui said the secrets were there, but then she'd said that roses made her sight better. Gypsy thought she'd figured it all out that evening when she determined that the secret was merely that she was alone and could think. But she'd been wrong. The secret was that you listen to what your heart has to say. Really listen. Put aside prejudice. Push those chips off the shoulders. Not try to convince the heart to believe what you want, but believe and trust in its judgment.

Could she do it? Gypsy shook her head. She was a strong woman with rock-hard determination, but she couldn't do what Willow was willing to do. She couldn't. Her Mexican pride, mixed up with all that stubborn Dulan blood she'd learned about, wouldn't let her chase after a man who wouldn't fight a legion of devils for her hand. No, she'd forget him.

And that was the last word. The very last one. She eased back into her bedroll, shut her eyes and willed herself to sleep. Tomorrow would begin a long, hot journey with little water. She needed her rest.

* * *

Hank arose an hour before daybreak, made a pot of coffee and leaned against his saddle to ponder the day. For the next week, tempers would probably flare at times. The land was flat but water would be non-existent. Thank goodness Homer would keep them all entertained in the evenings with his tales of the town they were headed toward. Hank was glad Tavish had chosen to go away without a big show. Merry didn't need that after all she'd been through. Hank's gut tightened when he thought of some other man raising that girl with Annie.

It had begun to look like the Dulan women were just along for insurance after all. He hadn't lost another woman since the one died with the fever that attacked Velvet. He was glad Velvet had survived and was happily married. He'd met Dr. Hoyt Baxter the year before when he took a wagon train of families to Oregon, and he was a good man. He found himself feeling sorry for the fellow who drew one of the Dulan's names if they did have to marry up with someone. Lord, it would take a big man to tame that Garnet, or Gussie. And Gypsy. Oh, my. What a woman! Riding off like that bareback to stampede the Indians' ponies. Why, even Bobby wouldn't ride that big black horse, and according to what Tavish said, Gypsy had even done stunts on the back of the feisty animal.

He'd thought at one time he might lose her to Tavish O'Leary. That they had something between them was no secret, but apparently they'd gotten it out of their systems all right, because Gypsy was still with the wagons and Tavish had no doubt reunited with his family by now.

He fumbled for his glasses in his shirt pocket when he heard someone approaching. The women still slept over at the circle so he wondered if it might be Bobby, coming in after a late night of scouting. However, he wasn't one bit surprised when he got his spectacles adjusted and looked up.

"Hello, Gypsy, I've been expecting you," he said, a smile covering his face.

## *Chapter Sixteen*

Tavish awoke to the crowing of the roosters, the brisk fall air promising very few more sultry hot days as it ruffled the starched and ironed curtains in his bedroom window, and a hurt so deep in his chest he couldn't even cry. He'd made the biggest mistake in his whole life, and they were grazing on the good grass in the pasture land of his very own ranch. He should have taken that money and bought the contract from Hank. Or at least offered to do so and then asked Gypsy Rose Dulan to go with him to Chalk Creek and be a helpmate for him the rest of his life.

But he hadn't, and now it was too late. He had no money to buy the contract, and besides, even if he did, there was no guarantee she wanted an Irish horse rancher when she could wait another few weeks and have so much more. Besides, there was that Irish pride he'd been born with and cultivated so thoroughly his whole life. Well, all that integrity and pride was going to make cold bed partners the rest of his life.

He hauled himself up out of bed, went out to milk the cow, and take care of the livestock his brothers and families had pitched in and cared for these past weeks he'd been gone. He'd missed the routine of tending his own ranch and animals and talked to them as he worked. He told the cow what a stupid owner she had; reminded the hogs that they were smarter than he was; and argued with the plow mules that he could have never lived with her anyway. By the time he finished the chores and was back in the cabin he'd convinced himself that he'd done the right thing, even though the words echoed in the still, small empty place where his heart used to live.

After a breakfast of pancakes covered with syrup he'd brewed on the back of the stove with a little sugar and water, he carefully dressed for church. Like always, he'd ride his horse over to the Flying Shamrock, his parents' ranch adjoining his own land, and they'd go together in the buggy to Chalk Creek for mass. He'd get used to the rut again and in it he'd find peace. It might take a while, he told himself, as he shaved in front of the small mirror above his chest of drawers. And if he didn't, he would just have to learn to live with the decisions he'd made.

Gypsy had brought colors to his life that he'd never experienced. Red for the anger they'd both shared because they'd fought so hard against their own hearts. Blue for the color of her strange eyes. Not sky-blue, not the blue of the bed where the stars twinkled, but the faint color of a robin's egg. Yellow for her laughter, because when she smiled and giggled the whole world lit up. Black for the fear in her eyes when the big cat was about to pounce on her. Orange when she screamed like a banshee as she stampeded those Indian ponies. All the colors combined into a kaleidoscope of brilliance when their lips touched.

He knotted the string tie at his neck, adjusted the collar of his snow-white, starched shirt with his finger, and donned his black hat. Maybe he wouldn't remember her anymore when he was a hundred years old. But he doubted that. Because he figured he'd still remember Gypsy Rose and see her blue eyes and black hair on his death bed. His last words would most likely be her name escaping his lips in a deep sigh.

His parents were loading children and grandchildren into

three buggies when he arrived. A place was made beside his mother for him and he left his horse tied to the hitching rail in the back of a rambling ranch-house with a wide, sweeping verandah around three sides. In the evening, his mother and father sat out there in their rocking chairs, holding hands and enjoying what they'd built with their own hands.

"So my son, why the long face? You have realized your dream with this trip. You have your own herd and everything you have is paid for. In a few years, your spread will overshadow ours," she patted his hand.

"Aye, Ma. I have that. It cost me too much, but I have it," he said soberly.

"Do you feel the O'Reilys overcharged you?" his mother asked.

"No, Ma. I overcharged me. Someday I will explain it all to you, but today I can not. It hurts my heart too bad to talk about it."

"I see," she said. So her son had fallen in love and the woman didn't return that love. It was written all over his face and etched into the sadness so deep in his dark eyes.

Tavish hopped out of the buggy when they reached the Catholic church on the corner of Main and Elm Streets, and helped his mother down, watching her fumble with the black lace covering her head as she climbed the steps into the church. A tingle played tag up and down his backbone, like it did when Gypsy was close by. He shaded his eyes with the back of his hand and looked up and down the street, but there was no one around. Not that Gypsy would be riding down the streets of Chalk Creek anyway. He might not utter her name after all when he was taking his last breath. By then he might be stone-cold crazy just thinking about her every day.

Gypsy rode into Chalk Creek that morning without even knowing it was Sunday. Not until she saw buggies in front of church-house buildings. She noticed a Methodist church on Main Street. A small white clapboard building with a bell tower that someone was ringing. She passed a Catholic church and noticed a large family going inside. As she rounded the side of the church, sitting on a corner lot, she found herself looking over the horses hitched outside. No, Tavish's horse wasn't there. What would she have done if it had been? Would she have walked right down the aisle and had a confrontation with him right there before the priest and God, Himself?

She smiled at that idea. Tavish stuttering and stammering around while she yelled at him, with her hands on her hips like a common fish wife. His whole family thinking she was a squaw in her leather riding skirt with fringe on the hem. It could be a real Sunday sideshow.

She passed a small school. Would they need a teacher there if Tavish sent her packing? Or would there be a horse ranch close by Chalk Creek where she could work as a groomer? The town was a typical small town. Not so very different from the one she visited when they went to town in Texas. A general store, a dressmaker, a bank, a hotel. Did they have a piano in the saloon over there, she wondered? Maybe Garnet would come back to Chalk Creek if she didn't marry a man in California.

A gray-haired lady walked down the wooden sidewalk, her heels making a rat-a-tat sound that Gypsy heard over the top of the busy noise of a Sunday morning. "Excuse me, ma'am," Gypsy said. "Could you tell me where the O'Leary ranch might be?"

"Why?" The older lady stopped and stared at her.

"Because I'm hunting for it," Gypsy said.

"You a Indian?"

"No, I'm a Mexican."

"Oh, well, whatever you are, you sure are a pretty thing. Which O'Leary you lookin' for. There's a tribe of them."

"Tavish, and thank you for the compliment."

"Tavish O'Leary, huh? Well, that's surely one to be hunting for, I'm telling you. A fine Irishman, that Tavish is. He just now got home from his last wagon train run. Bought the last of his herd from me and my husband. Good boy, that Tavish is. But as full of blarney as a full-blooded Irish," the woman laughed. "Well, now you keep going down this road until you reach a fork in the road. Right one would take you to the older boys' ranches. Left one takes you to the Flying Shamrock. That's his folks' place. You just ride right on past it. Road will kind of peter out about there, but there's a path on down another half a mile. At the end of that path is Tavish's place. A little whitewashed cabin with a big front porch. Couple of hounds but they won't hurt you."

"Thank you," Gypsy said.

"Didn't catch your name," the lady said.

"I'm Gypsy Rose Dulan," Gypsy drew herself up tall in the saddle and announced without stuttering.

"Well, I'm Bertha O'Reily and welcome to Chalk Creek. I got a horse ranch with my husband out east of town. We been running that ranch since the day we married more'n thirty years ago. You come and see me if you need anything. I like the way you handle that big old horse you're riding."

"Thank you again."

She rode past the front of the O'Leary home and looked, but she didn't see the big red horse there either. Maybe he hadn't attended church this morning after all. Lots of things could keep a man home from church, especially one with animals. She found the cabin Bertha told her about and sure enough, two oversized hounds came out to greet her. She rubbed their ears when she'd dismounted and looped the reins over the hitching post in front of the house. Rambling red rose bushes climbed up the end porch posts. The cooler weather of late had given it a burst of life and although it wasn't covered like it would be in spring, it still had a few buds as well as full-blown roses to offer that morning. The scent wafted across the porch and filled her nostrils as she knocked on the door, tried to ease the pounding of her heart, and waited.

No answer. She went to the back door and knocked harder. Still no answer. She spotted a barn and set a straight path for it. Tavish wasn't there, but everything was clean and well tended. Not a thing out of place or in disarray. Her grandfather would like the looks of this place. Nice and neat, even if was on a small scale. A look out the back door of the barn widened her eyes. It was paradise. A picture of the promised land more pure than anything she could have ever imagined. The most beautiful horses she'd ever laid eyes on grazed contentedly in the fenced pasture out there. She blinked, expecting it to change.

It didn't.

She found the hog lot, the chicken pens, the milking shed, even the smokehouse. All tended immaculately. She went back to the front door and knocked again, but there was still no answer. This time she wasn't a bit surprised. She opened the front door, took her hat off and hung it on the peg behind the door right beside his work hat. Then she set about prowling through his cabin.

Starched curtains on the windows. A feminine touch for sure brought there by his sisters or his mother. Leftover pancakes on the stove warmer. She picked up two; one for each hand and ate as she stood in the doorway to the bedroom and looked at the big four-poster bed and matching chest of drawers. The smell of his shaving soap still floated through the morning air and she inhaled deeply. If she'd had any doubts about her decision to leave the train, they were gone now. She'd convince him to lay aside all that Irish integrity if it took a solid year. She'd sure enough had to lay aside what dignity she had when she walked into the men's camp early that morning.

She'd gone with what little money she had in her trunk to plead with Hank to release her from the contract. She'd walk to Chalk Creek. It was only eight miles from where they were camped. She could make it by nightfall quite easily, she'd told him. But Hank had just laughed, assuring her that she wasn't going to have a husband at the end of the trip after all because he really thought they were going to be a woman or two long anyway. Besides, Jake had been his friend for years and he wanted Jake's daughters to be settled and happy. So she was released from the contract without a fight and without money changing hands.

Then the bargaining began for the black horse. That was a different matter. Hank drove a hard bargain. Equally as hard as the one he'd driven with Willow when she needed a horse. When it was finished she had five dollars left, but she owned the big, ill-tempered animal, and a saddle. She'd filled the saddlebags with what she could, gave the rest to her sisters, kissed them good-bye amidst a flurry of tears and instructions, and rode off.

And she'd done the right thing.

She knew it in her heart because there was peace there. She'd found her promised land in Utah Territory and hopefully in Tavish O'Leary's heart.

Tavish begged out of lunch with his family. If he had to look at happily married people he'd gag. He kissed his mother on the forehead, retrieved his horse from the back yard and rode away, waving at his uncle one last time as he went.

He saw the big black horse tethered to the hitching post when he rounded the last curve. It looked somewhat like that horse Gypsy rode but this one was saddled. Then again it looked like the one that Meggie McDougal rode sometimes. Now what would that red-haired woman be doing at his place on a Sunday morning after church? To be sure he'd flirted with her a time or two, but he didn't want to see her this day.

He didn't take the time to put his own horse in the barn, but looped the reins around the post and took the porch steps two at a time. He burst through the front door to find

Gypsy, the sunlight pouring in the window of his bedroom and silhouetting her in the doorway.

"Hello, little Irish boy," she said simply. The faint aroma of roses preceded him into the house. It had been there all along and her heart had screamed at her to open her eyes and see it; roses did enhance the power just like Paqui had said. And every time she'd used them, Tavish was there. She just hadn't realized he'd been the answer. Not until now when she looked across the room and her heart stood perfectly still.

"Squaw?" he said hoarsely, surprised that he could even get that word out of a mouth so dry it felt as if it had been swabbed with cotton balls. Faith and saints, but she was lovely standing there in his bedroom door. He'd never dared hope she would come to him once he left the wagon train, yet, there she was. Was he dreaming? If he walked across the room and gathered her into his arms would she disappear?

"I've come to tell you that you are a pig-headed Irishman. That you are full of blarney and you are too full of pride, and if you ever call me squaw again I will slit your throat and enjoy watching you die," she said coldly, ice dripping from every word.

"And?" his eyes twinkled.

"And *te quiero*, which means 'I love you' in Spanish," she said, softly. "Heaven help me Tavish but I do. Hank has released me from the contract, and I bought that horse out there from him. You can throw me out or marry me, but I'm . . ."

"Are you proposing to me?" he asked.

"I am," she said.

"Then I accept." he crossed the room and drew her close to his chest. She didn't disappear but rather snuggled down, fitting there perfectly. "*Taim i' ngra leat,* that means 'I love you' in Irish," he said, tilting her head back to look deeply into those lovely blue eyes. "I was a fool. The horses could have waited for another year."

"Yes, you were, and they could have, but I won't hold that against you if you'll kiss me."

"Yes, ma'am," he whispered as he bent to claim not only her mouth, but her heart and soul for his own.

"And so what do we do now?" she asked with a nervous giggle, the bed behind her, her future bright in front of her.

"Well, did you bring that pretty blue dress of yours in the saddle bags?"

"Yes."

"Then put it on and we shall hitch up the buggy and go to the Flying Shamrock, my folks' place down the road a bit. My uncle is there. He only comes to visit our little church in Chalk Creek a few times a year. Mostly we have our own priest but today he came because he hadn't seen me in a while."

Tavish led her out to the porch, not wanting to let go of her hand even for a minute.

"What's your uncle got to do with my blue dress?"

"Father Douglas Flannigan. He is my mother's youngest brother and he is a priest. I'm sure he can marry us this afternoon."

"Oh, Tavish," she threw her arms around his neck. "I've really found my promised land."

"Aye, you have. But even in the Good Book, they had to fight to keep the promised land once they laid claim to it, darlin'." He could scarcely believe that God had smiled on him with such a blessing that day.

"Then we will fight," she said, pulling his mouth down to hers one more time before she changed into her wedding dress. "Together, Tavish, we will fight for our promised land. I love you."

"And I love you," Tavish said, carrying in her saddlebags with one hand. His other firmly around her waist. "And I'm sure we will fight each other together for a long time."

"Forever," she said, a twinkle in her blue eyes as they went back inside the cabin together.